"I mean nothing to you, nor you to me," said Antonia.

"You are my wife. The marriage was not of my seeking, but since you now bear my name, you will conduct yourself becomingly. If you do not, I promise that you will most bitterly regret it."

For a few seconds the dark eyes met and held the blue, and it was as though swords had been crossed in the quiet room. Then Antonia, trembling with anger, moved forward until she stood within a yard of Geraint.

"Do not try me too far," she said in a low fierce voice. "I can be a dangerous enemy, for I have been taught only too well how to hate."

Laughter leapt into his eyes again, and the brief moment of seriousness was past. "Then it is time you were taught to love," Geraint replied.

Fawcett Crest Books
by Sylvia Thorpe:

THE SCANDALOUS LADY ROBIN

CAPTAIN GALLANT

ROMANTIC LADY

THE RELUCTANT ADVENTURESS

TARRINGTON CHASE

THE SCARLET DOMINO

THE SCAPEGRACE

THE SILVER NIGHTINGALE

Sylvia Thorpe

The SCARLET DOMINO

A FAWCETT CREST BOOK

Fawcett Publications, Inc., Greenwich, Connecticut

THE SCARLET DOMINO

A Fawcett Crest Book reprinted by arrangement with Hurst &
Blackett, Ltd.

Printed in Canada

First printing: November 1975

The
SCARLET DOMINO

Part One

The room was as cold as death, in spite of the major part of two tree-trunks burning in the great hooded hearth, for it was an apartment of vast proportions, dwarfing even the huge four-poster bed which occupied a dais in the middle of the floor. The windows were tightly shut, so that the roar of the wind in the woods which encircled the house was muted to a long-drawn, ceaseless sigh, but the heavy curtains stirred constantly in icy currents of air. Candles in wall-sconces illuminated a portrait above the hearth, and, with the leaping flames below, provided the only light, so that the far reaches of the room were lost in shadow.

In that patch of brightness near the fire, six people were gathered. The aged master of the house, propped up with pillows in a big armchair, a fur rug about his lower limbs; his steward and housekeeper, summoned there to act as witnesses; his chaplain, who was performing the marriage ceremony; and the bride and groom, who had met for the first time ten minutes before that ceremony began.

". . . an honourable estate, instituted by God . . . ordained for the mutual society, help and comfort the one ought to have of the other . . ." The bride shivered, fighting an impulse to cry out in protest. Ordained by God? No, ordained by the despotic, half-crazy will of Sir Charles Kelshall, her grandfather, to satisfy the hatred which ruled his life. Little comfort she could look to give or to find in a marriage such as this, to a stranger who had to be bribed to wed her.

She stole a glance at the young man beside her, and though she was a tall girl, she had to look up to see his face. He was staring straight ahead, his profile clearly outlined against the shadows beyond; straight nose and resolute chin; a hard, reckless mouth; fair hair with a glint of gold, plainly dressed and caught back at the nape of his neck by a broad black ribbon. His whole appearance was one of careless elegance, and she would never have guessed, had she not been told, that less than two weeks ago he had been in the Common Debtors' Ward of Newgate Gaol. "A bridegroom handsome enough to please any woman," her grandfather had told her callously. "Think yourself lucky, my girl! I could so easily have married you to a man old or misshapen." She had not been deceived. Sir Charles had found her a young, vigorous husband for one reason only; that there might be children of the union, lawful children to inherit the wealth he guarded so jealously.

". . . forsaking all others . . ." Again the silent cry of protest rose up within her, the rebellious culmination of a lifetime of fruitless rebellion. This time she almost uttered it; would have uttered it had she not been conscious of Sir Charles's gaze upon her. The pale blue eyes, sunken amid wrinkled, yellow skin yet blazing with grotesque vitality, warned her that rebellion now would end as it had always done, in humiliation and defeat.

". . . for better, for worse, for richer, for poorer . . ." He would be rich, this pauper her grandfather had bought. Richer by her own impressive dowry now, and by the Kelshall estate and fortune when the old man died. No wonder he had agreed to the infamous bargain. As though the voice belonged to someone else, she heard herself making the responses, the empty promises to love and honour and obey.

"With this ring, I thee wed . . ." The slim band of gold was a fetter, chaining her to the future Sir Charles had decreed, a future which took no account of her own hopes and dreams and fears, for when had these ever mattered to him? When had she ever mattered, except as a pawn in his interminable game of hatred and vengeance?

". . . with all my worldly goods I thee endow." Now she felt an hysterical desire to laugh, for surely it was she who should be speaking those words? She whose worldly goods had trapped her into this travesty of marriage. What a hideous mockery it was, these vows of love and fidelity between two strangers. No, it was worse than mockery; it was blasphemy.

The chaplain pronounced them man and wife, the blessing and the prayers were spoken, and the ceremony which, on that cold February night in 1761, bound Antonia Kelshall and Geraint St. Arvan to one another for the rest of their lives was over.

St. Arvan was in a curious frame of mind, compounded almost equally of anger, shame and uneasiness. Until his arrival at Kelshall Park earlier that evening, he had had no idea what would be required of him. The chaplain, Edward Thornbury, had come to him in Newgate with the astonishing information that Sir Charles Kelshall, of whom until that moment Geraint had never heard, had settled all his debts and, being now his only creditor, was

prepared to cancel the obligation in return for some un-
specified service. A service, Mr. Thornbury had hastened
to add, which was in no way contrary to the Law.

Geraint was naturally suspicious. How, he inquired,
had an old gentleman who, according to Thornbury, was
bedridden somewhere in the depths of Gloucestershire,
informed himself so particularly about a complete stranger? How, in fact, had he known of that stranger's existence?

The chaplain's answer to that was frank enough. "I, sir,
was his informant. I was born on the St. Arvan estate,
though I left it in your grandfather's time. My sister,
however, still lives there, and from her I learned of your
misfortune. I hope to serve you as well as Sir Charles,
who has been my patron for more than thirty years."

"Then serve me to some purpose, Mr. Thornbury, and
tell me exactly what it is your patron requires of me."

"I regret, sir, that I am not at liberty to disclose more
than I have already told you. Sir Charles's commands on
that score were explicit. If you wish to be free, you must
undertake to do without question whatever Sir Charles
demands."

For some moments after he had spoken, there was silence in the gloomy chamber where the interview was
taking place. At last Geraint found his voice.

"You cannot be serious! Am I to pledge myself blindly
to some unnamed task at the bidding of a man I have
never met? I thank you, no!"

He turned abruptly away, took a couple of strides to
the small, barred window, and stood staring out into the
glimmer of wintry dusk beyond. Unless Thornbury were
mad or lying, the way of freedom was opening before
him, but there was some flaw in the miracle. There must
be. Fortune simply did not bestow favours so lavishly
upon a man and demand nothing in return. Yet what

price could be too great to pay for escape from Newgate? He heard Thornbury say:

"Permit me to remark, sir, that I find your hesitation curious, and in no way consistent with the traditions of your family, or your own reputation."

"The wild St. Arvans, eh?" Geraint turned to face him; there was a hint of rueful humour in his voice. "Yes, we have a name for recklessness and folly, and I have done as much as any of us to keep the tradition alive. Observe, however, whither it has brought me. Is it so strange that I should have learned a measure of caution?"

"'If recklessness brought you to Newgate, Mr. St. Arvan, caution seems likely to keep you here. May I ask, sir, how old you are?"

"Nine-and-twenty." Geraint looked faintly surprised, but then he laughed shortly. "I understand you! If I refuse Sir Charles's bargain I may rot here for years."

He paused, forcing himself to face again what that would mean. He had endured it for three months, the dirt and the degradation, the utter hopelessness of this place of lost souls, and it had come near to breaking him. Now he was offered escape from it. His new-found caution, the more easily defeated because it was foreign to his true nature, was not proof against the temptation placed before him.

"So be it," he said with a shrug. "I accept your patron's offer, Mr. Thornbury. How soon can you arrange my release?"

"I will set about it at once. Not a moment shall be wasted." Mr. Thornbury got up briskly from the bench where he had been sitting, but then hesitated, coughed, and finally said rather awkwardly: "There is just one thing, Mr. St. Arvan. Sir Charles insists that, before you are released, you sign a note-of-hand for the sum he has expended on your behalf."

Geraint took this aspersion on his good faith with equanimity. "He overlooks nothing, does he?" he said cheerfully. "I begin to have considerable respect for Sir Charles Kelshall."

That respect endured only until he was face to face with his benefactor, and learned from him the exact nature of the service demanded. Sir Charles, totally unmoved by the young man's angry astonishment, deigned neither to plead nor to argue. He simply issued an ultimatum; either St. Arvan married Miss Kelshall immediately—Mr. Thornbury had obtained a special license in London—or be returned to Newgate. Geraint, furious but baffled, agreed.

When the brief formalities had been concluded, Sir Charles dismissed his companions in the peremptory fashion which seemed habitual with him.

"Leave me now." His voice was a mere thread of sound in the big, quiet room. "Not you, St. Arvan! I want to talk to you." He watched chaplain, steward and housekeeper file meekly away, and then turned his malevolent gaze towards his granddaughter. "Why do you linger? I bade you go."

He spoke as he had spoken to the servants, but though a faint tinge of colour rose in the creamy pallor of her cheeks, she made no response. She simply curtsied very formally and turned away, her satin skirts making a faint whispering sound against the polished floor as she crossed the room. St. Arvan moved quickly to open the door for her, but she did not acknowledge his presence by so much as a glance as she went past him.

He closed the door and returned slowly to Sir Charles, marvelling, as he had marvelled since the first moment of setting eyes on the old man, that life could still linger in so shrunken and wasted a frame. Kelshall's coat of black velvet hung in folds upon him; the hands emerging from the ruffles of fine lace were emaciated yellow claws; his face, between the powdered curls of his wig, with its shrunken features and parchment-like skin, seemed already to have been touched by the finger of death. Only his eyes, of a blue so light that it was almost colourless, yet oddly brilliant, seemed alive; living eyes in the face of a corpse. The contrast filled Geraint with a revulsion which he had to make a conscious effort to conceal.

"It is very well," the old man said as St. Arvan paused beside his chair. "Very well!" He thrust a tremulous hand into the breast of his coat and drew out a folded paper. "Take this, and cast it into the fire."

Geraint accepted the paper and unfolded it. It was the note-of-hand he had signed in Newgate.

"Cast it into the fire," Sir Charles repeated. "The debt has been paid."

After a moment's hesitation Geraint obeyed, but as the paper crumbled into ashes he said coldly:

"I have done what you asked of me, Sir Charles. Is it not time I was told the reason for it?"

Even though he asked the question, he believed that he already knew the answer. Waiting for his bride to appear, he had wondered apprehensively if she would prove to be hideously disfigured or deformed, but Antonia Kelshall was strikingly beautiful, with the figure and bearing of a classical goddess. Heavy waves of jet-black hair framed a proud, oval face with great dark eyes and a tragic mouth —a sombre, un-English loveliness such as he had never seen. So the only other likely explanation, he had reflected furiously, must be the correct one. Wealthy, titled gentlemen did not hurry their grand-daughters into secret marriage with a stranger unless there were some pressingly urgent reason.

Sir Charles was nodding slowly. "You may know the reason, St. Arvan—now. It is murder!"

The word, with all its monstrous implications, dropped softly into the silence, yet seemed to Geraint to echo and re-echo around the room. He stared, dumbfounded, at Sir Charles, and the old man looked back at him with sardonic comprehension.

"You imagined, of course, that I had gone to these lengths merely so that you should provide a name for some other man's by-blow," he said contemptuously. "Be easy, St. Arvan! Your bride is virtuous. I have had too close a watch kept upon her for it to be otherwise."

"I am relieved to hear it," Geraint replied ironically. "Permit me to observe, however, that I would find that explanation more credible than the one you offer."

"Murder!" Kelshall repeated obstinately. "Murder twenty years old and still unpunished." He lifted a trembling hand to point to the portrait above the hearth; his feeble voice shook with emotion. "My son! My Anthony, butchered when he was barely two-and-twenty! Killed because he was my heir! But I cheated the man who killed him, and I'll cheat him yet again before I die."

Geraint glanced briefly at the portrait, of a fair-haired youth with a weak, discontented face and the same piercing yet colourless eyes as Sir Charles, and then he looked again at the old man. He was sure now that Kelshall was not normal. Complete sanity did not look out of those awful eyes, and no sane man would have created this fantastic situation. A faint understanding of the twisted reasoning behind it was dawning in his mind, but there was still a great deal which puzzled him.

"Let me be sure, sir, that I understand you," he said. "Your son, you say, was murdered by someone who thought to profit by the crime, but the inheritance which should have been Anthony Kelshall's went instead to his daughter—of whose existence, presumably, the murderer was unaware. Do you fear for *her* life, now that increasing years make it difficult for you to protect her?"

The old man's strong emotion seemed to have subsided. He looked at Geraint with mocking eyes, and was shaken by soundless, uncanny laughter.

"If I did, St. Arvan, I would fear no longer. It is your life, not Antonia's, which henceforth will be in danger."

"Mine?" In spite of his anger and perplexity, Geraint laughed. "Gad's life! Is that why you tricked me into this marriage? To provide a decoy to draw danger away from her?"

"No!" With another lightning change of mood, the feeble voice and glaring eyes were filled with the bitterest contempt. "I care no more for her safety than for yours, save that your lives are important to my purpose. My only concern is to ensure that not a penny of my money falls into Roger Kelshall's hands."

"Roger Kelshall?" Geraint repeated incredulously. "You suspect *him* of being guilty of your son's murder?"

"I know that he is guilty of it," Sir Charles replied flatly. "Are you acquainted with him?"

Geraint shrugged. "Scarcely that. I have some slight acquaintance with his son, Vincent."

Watching the old man, he saw an expression he could not interpret gleam for an instant in the extraordinary eyes, and then the wrinkled lids drooped suddenly. Sir Charles stretched out a claw-like hand and tinkled the silver bell which stood on a small table beside him.

"I am very tired now, but we shall talk of this again tomorrow." He shook once more with that weird, silent laughter. "You may go, St. Arvan. Your bride is waiting."

Antonia, dismissed so curtly from her grandfather's presence, made her way slowly to the library in the west wing of the house. Most of the formal reception rooms at Kelshall Park were closed, for it was five years since Sir Charles had left his bedchamber, and even before that he had neither paid nor received social calls. So it was in the library, or in a small parlour, once the schoolroom, on the second floor, that his grand-daughter spent most of her time.

Tonight her choice of the library was deliberate. Her first impulse had been to seek refuge in the parlour, but that, with her bedchamber which adjoined it, was the only corner of the great house where she had any degree of privacy, which could in any way be regarded as home, and the thought of receiving there the stranger who was now her husband filled her with repugnance. The other thought, that through Sir Charles's scheming, St. Arvan had the right to enter either room, she thrust to the back of her mind. To dwell upon that was to give way to the panic welling up within her, and fear was the one thing she was determined not to betray.

Entering the library, she walked across to the fire and stood staring down at the flickering flames, then, becoming aware that this was the only light in the room, went to tug angrily at the bell-rope. When a footman answered the summons she said imperiously:

"Why is this room in darkness? Light the candles immediately. All of them."

He kindled a taper at the fire and moved about the room, while Antonia, sitting now in a high-backed chair by the fireplace, watched the light slowly brighten on the books and pictures and tried to remain indifferent to the servant's knowing, curious glance. All the servants at Kelshall Park accorded her the outward indications of respect, but they were very well aware how her grandfather regarded her, and made that awareness clear to her in subtle ways. They resented having to wait upon her, and she had no doubt that they were gloating now over the situation in which she found herself.

When the man had gone she got up and began to move restlessly about the room, too agitated to remain still. The events of the evening had the unreality of a remembered nightmare. It seemed impossible that she was married, bound for life to a man of whose existence she had been unaware only an hour or so ago, but the ring on her finger was a reality which could not be denied, symbol of a tyranny of which she would never be free. Her grandfather had not much longer to live, but he had passed his authority over her to a man of his own choice, and the dreams she had lately dared to cherish, of an escape to freedom and happiness, could never be fulfilled.

The door was thrown suddenly open by the footman who had lighted the candles, and St. Arvan came past him into the room. Antonia, turning sharply towards them, caught a glimpse of the smirk on the servant's face as he withdrew, and her panic was overwhelmed for an instant by a spurt of pure anger. She directed at Geraint a look of such blazing hatred that even he, prepared for hostility, was startled, and then she turned her back on him and pretended to be absorbed in selecting a book from among the volumes lining the walls. Geraint walked across to the fireplace and stood there, thoughtfully regarding her. When the silence had lasted for the greater part of a minute he said quietly:

"This is a devilish odd situation, madam, in which we find ourselves. Is it too much to hope that you are more fully acquainted with the reasons for it than I?"

He thought for a moment that she was not going to answer him. Then, without moving, she said scornfully: "To be sure! 'Without question' was your bargain with Sir Charles, was it not?"

He was taken aback. "You know that?"

She lifted a book from one of the shelves and turned at last to face him. Her eyes met his with a contempt she did not try to disguise, and then her glance travelled over him from head to foot, returning eventually to his face. She made a little gesture of disdain.

"It is a singular experience," she said coldly. "Not many women, I feel sure, have had their husbands purchased for them from the wards of Newgate Prison."

The colour rose in his cheeks beneath the lash of words and look, but he did not hesitate to hit back. "Perhaps not, madam, but since you agreed to such a course it scarcely becomes you to complain of it."

"*I* agree to it?" She took a step forward, her eyes flashing. "Do you dare to suppose that I knew what was intended?"

"Did you not? When you spoke of my bargain with Sir Charles I assumed that you knew and approved of what he had done."

"You were wrong," she said deliberately. "He told me of it not an hour before that damnable ceremony took place."

"Good God!" He looked blankly at her, and then a swift frown came. "But you agreed to the marriage."

"Yes!" There was a world of bitterness in Antonia's voice. "I agreed! I have learned to my cost that one does not with impunity defy Sir Charles."

He continued to frown at her for a second or two, and then turned away to pace the length of the room, hands clasped behind him and his chin sunk upon the fine lace at his throat. Antonia watched him with an uneasiness which while he was not looking at her she did not attempt to disguise, for the thought had flashed frighteningly into her mind that Geraint St. Arvan, too, was a man it might not be wise to defy.

There was a dangerous quality about him which was hard to define, compounded as it was of a number of small things. The set of his wide shoulders beneath the plum-coloured velvet coat; the way he moved, with a kind of lazy strength which held a suggestion of latent power; the cast of the handsome, reckless face, with those intensely blue eyes, and a mouth which, even if less hard than she had at first thought, indicated that here was a man accustomed to getting his own way. Yet might she not have known it would be so? Her grandfather was bound to have chosen a husband for her as ruthless as he was himself.

"Can you tell me the meaning of this rigmarole of avarice and murder Sir Charles talks of?" Geraint, pausing again beside her, spoke abruptly. "He says that his cousin, Roger Kelshall, killed your father in the hope of inheriting a fortune."

Antonia shrugged, moving away from him to seat herself beside the fire. "That is what he believes. Roger Kelshall killed my father in a duel before I was born. Sir Charles looks upon it as deliberate murder for the sake of gain."

"But Roger Kelshall is a rich man."

"He is now. His present wealth came to him with his second wife. At the time of Anthony Kelshall's death he had little enough. Sir Charles had married late in life, and his wife died giving birth to their son. It is said that he worshipped her, and that after her death all his love was centred upon the child." She shrugged again. "If that is true, whatever affection of which he was capable died with his son. Since that time his whole life has been governed by hatred, and he has lived for one thing only—to thwart his kinsman's supposed design upon the Kelshall fortune. That is the only use he has ever had for me. The only reason he adopted me at all."

"Adopted you?" Geraint looked at her in astonishment. "But you are Anthony Kelshall's daughter!"

There was a moment's silence, while Antonia stared at

him with a bitter satisfaction dawning in her eyes. "So he did not tell you everything," she said at length, and laughed softly. "You fool, why do you suppose he had to go to such lengths to find a husband for his heiress? I am Anthony Kelshall's daughter—by a gipsy girl he met at a Michaelmas fair."

Now, to Geraint, many things were suddenly made plain. It was an age when, among the nobility and gentry, birth counted for as much, if not more, than fortune, and though illegitimacy in itself might be no great hardship, parentage such as Antonia had just confessed to so defiantly was a different matter. Not just base-born, but half gipsy! What man of good family would take such a wife, heiress or no, especially when the imprint of her mother's people was set so clearly upon face and figure?

Looking at her, Geraint wondered why he had not guessed it from the first. The aquiline features, black hair and dark eyes, the proud and graceful carriage which was as natural as breathing—he had seen these more than once among the dark, secret Romany folk who roamed the roads and were to be found at any county fair. He had noticed beautiful women among them, but in Antonia that beauty was softened and refined, partly, no doubt, by heredity, and even more by the nature of her upbringing. She was one of the loveliest women he had ever seen, lovely enough to bemuse any man's senses, but—base-born and half gipsy.

And he was married to her. Fury at the way in which he had been tricked flared up within him, for no matter to what straits he had been reduced he was still a man of his times, with a deep, enduring pride in an ancient name. He had always regarded it as his eventual duty to marry, that the name might be carried on; now he had been trapped, by Sir Charles's twisted schemes and his own desperate need, into the kind of misalliance upon which his own class looked askance, and into which he would never have entered of his own free will.

"Then I am astonished, madam, that you complain of the provision Sir Charles has made for you," he said savagely. "He was prudent to keep his own counsel. Had I known the truth . . . !"

"You would have preferred to remain in Newgate rather than take me for your wife!" Antonia's scorn and anger equalled his own. "The thought of freedom would not have tempted you, nor the chance to squander my fortune as you have squandered your own. Do you expect me to believe that? Do you really believe it yourself?"

The taunt, and the utter contempt in her voice and eyes, brought him up short in spite of his anger. Did he believe it? If all the facts had been set before him, would he have sent Thornbury away disappointed, and stayed in the filth and squalor of Newgate rather than marry this girl who looked at him with such hostility as she flung down her scornful challenge? A certain humorous self-knowledge which was a saving grace of his nature told him that he would not.

"No, perhaps not," he said in a wry tone. "It is easy to say so now, but I think I would have taken any way of escape that offered. I did so, in fact, when I agreed to Sir Charles's proposal."

"What prisoner would not?" Antonia's voice was bitter, and she gazed into the fire with an expression which, he thought suddenly, had no place in a countenance as young as hers. "Do you think it is only in such places as Newgate that one may know the misery of perpetual imprisonment? I have known it all my life! This house my prison, and Sir Charles my gaoler. Now, because I shall soon be of age and he no longer able to keep me here against my will, he thrusts me into marriage with a man who has to be bribed to wed me. Thus he ensures that I shall never be free."

Geraint did not immediately reply. Hitherto self-absorbed, considering the situation only as it affected himself, he was now realising that Antonia was as much a victim of Sir Charles's demented plotting as he was. He still did not completely understand, but one thing, at least, was certain. The ceremony which had just been performed was legal and binding; he and Antonia were married, and nothing was to be gained by hurling insults at one another.

"Perhaps it would be as well if you told me the whole story," he said at length. "It is too late now for either of us to draw back, and a measure of frankness will probably serve us better than anything else."

She shrugged ungraciously. "There is little more to tell. Anthony Kelshall was on the point of being married—to a well-born, well-dowered bride of his father's choosing —when he met my mother, and created a local scandal by openly setting her up as his mistress. This led to an estrangement from his bride-to-be and a violent quarrel with Sir Charles, with the result that Anthony went off to London, and his light-o'-love with him.

"There, partly, I imagine, to spite his father, he struck up a close friendship with his cousin, Roger Kelshall. Sir Charles had always distrusted that branch of the family, who had been his heirs until Anthony was born, and he suspected Roger of desiring Anthony's death so that he might regain that position. Some months later his fears appeared to be justified, for news came that Anthony had been killed by Roger in a duel arising out of a quarrel over the card-table."

"A duel, properly conducted," Geraint pointed out, "can scarcely be regarded as murder."

"Sir Charles regarded it as such. He did everything in his power to have Roger brought to justice, but he had prudently gone abroad, and everyone, it seemed, believed that his accusation against Anthony, of cheating at cards, was fully justified.

"So Sir Charles turned his attention to thwarting his kinsman's supposed schemes. The gipsy girl, who was still with Anthony at the time of his death, was soon to bear his child, and Sir Charles resolved that that child should take its father's part as heir to the Kelshall fortune. He hoped for a grandson, a second Anthony, and his disappointment over that is one of the reasons he hates me. That, and the fact that I have grown up resembling my mother. He considers her, you see, to be as guilty as Roger Kelshall of his son's death."

Geraint was frowning. "You say that he hates you, yet he adopted you, had you educated, made you his heiress."

"What does that signify? There is no one else of his blood living, except Roger Kelshall and his family. He thought that the wealth I am to inherit would outweigh the facts of my birth, and that he would be able to arrange a marriage for me in keeping with the Kelshall pride. But he has ever made enemies more easily than friends, and the old scandal has never been allowed to die." She paused, looking at Geraint with no lessening of her defiant hostility. "Until tonight, I was glad of that!"

He let that pass. "What did you mean to do, when you come of age?"

"I was going to leave this house for ever!" Antonia rose suddenly to her feet and began to pace restlessly about the room, as though the thought of that intended escape and the manner in which it had been prevented was too galling to allow her to remain still. "I would have gone long since, but I knew that as long as it were in his power to do so, he would have me brought back, and I would have no stomach for the punishment I knew he would inflict upon me. So I forced myself to be patient, and lived for the day when I might claim my freedom."

Geraint, leaning against the side of the carved stone
fireplace, watched her in silence for a few moments, ap-
preciative of her grace, of the lithe vigour of her movements which not even the cumbersome hooped skirts of
her gown could entirely disguise. At last he said curiously:

"To claim freedom might have meant sacrificing everything else. Suppose the old man had disinherited you?"

"You think I would have cared if he did?" She halted,
and swung with a swirl of shimmering satin to face him.
Her voice shook with anger and disdain. "I hate the Kelshall fortune and all it stands for! I would a thousand
times rather be free and penniless, tramping the roads like
my mother's people, than an heiress imprisoned here in
the gloom and the shadows. Do you dare to doubt that?"

"I don't doubt that you believe it," he replied with
some amusement, "and had you lived so since infancy
you might have been happy enough. But a gipsy's life,
m'dear, would bear hard on a woman accustomed to live
well and lie soft, as you have always done."

"You would think that, of course," she retorted dis-
paragingly. "The mere fact that you are here proves that
material comfort means more to you than anything else."

"It means a deal more to me now than it did before my
stay in Newgate," he admitted frankly. "Until then I took
it for granted, as I fancy you have always done. It needs
an intimate acquaintance with poverty and hardship to
breed a proper respect for the good things of life." He
paused, studying her with mingled curiosity and disbelief.
"Were you seriously planning to go out into the world, to
fend for yourself without money or friends?"

She had been facing him defiantly, her whole attitude
eloquent of the same scorn which had rung through her
words, but now she turned suddenly away to restore to its
place, unopened, the book she had taken from the
shelves. Over her shoulder she said shortly:

"No price would be too high to pay for escape from this place and my grandfather's mad tyranny. I should not have starved, I assure you."

"That much, at least, is certain," he agreed dryly. "With your face and figure you would soon have found a protector. Yet I cannot help wondering why, if you were prepared to do that, you should now complain so bitterly of the present situation."

She turned slowly to face him again. Contempt was in the line of her lips, the slight, disdainful lifting of her black brows. "Are you trying to convince me," she said bitingly, "that there is any difference?"

For a second or two longer he continued to regard her, and then he strolled unhurriedly across to where she stood with her back to the rows of handsomely bound volumes. He leaned his left hand on the shelf close to her shoulder, and cupped the right lightly about her chin, so that she had no choice but to meet his eyes.

"Oh, a vast difference, m'dear," he said with a slight smile. "I happen to be your husband."

She stood rigid, scorning to make any attempt to break free, but in spite of her angry hostility, he read fear in the dark, defiant eyes. Unexpectedly, compassion shook him, and a sudden, angry self-disgust. His hand dropped to her wrist; he lifted it, and brushed her fingers gently with his lips.

"A situation to which we both need time to grow accustomed," he added lightly. "I look forward to our better acquaintance, but for the present, madam, permit me to bid you good night."

He released her hand and stepped back, bowed, and so left her. The door closed behind him, and Antonia stood leaning against the book-case, shaken with astonishment and relief, listening to his firm footsteps receding across the room beyond.

Sir Charles Kelshall was angry, and making no attempt to dissemble it. Propped against a mound of pillows in his enormous bed, looking more wizened and corpse-like by daylight than he had the previous night, he glared malevolently at Geraint as the young man came across the room towards him. Ignoring his courteous greeting, he said in a voice which rage rendered even more tremulous than usual:

"Are you trying to make a fool of me, St. Arvan? Don't think you can trifle with me simply because I let you burn that note-of-hand. Your fingers are not on the purse-strings yet!"

Geraint looked at him with faint surprise, finding that his first, instinctive dislike of the old man had in no way abated. He said coldly:

"I do not understand you, sir. Neither do I care to be addressed in that fashion."

"Like it or not, you'll bear with it, young man! And to help your understanding, let me tell you that I did not go to so much trouble and expense so that Antonia could be your wife in name alone."

"You are impatient, Sir Charles!" Geraint's voice had hardened, his manner become even more icily courteous than before. "Since I met your grand-daughter for the first time at the wedding ceremony, you can scarcely have expected me to be in such unseemly haste to claim my rights as her husband." He broke off, studying the old man's face with dawning disbelief. "Good God! You did expect it! Have you no consideration for her at all?"

"Consideration? For her?" The harsh whisper of Kelshall's voice throbbed with contempt. "Don't deceive yourself, St. Arvan! I have had her taught to look and speak like a lady, but at heart she is as much a gipsy drab as her mother was. You've no call to be delicate with her. Take her, humble her, break her spirit and teach her that you are the master!"

There was a pause before Geraint replied, during which he studied the old man with deepening disgust. Until that moment he had thought Antonia exaggerated when she said that her grandfather hated her, but now he knew it for the simple truth. Hatred, naked and undisguised, was in Sir Charles's voice and look as he uttered that callous advice—or did he intend it as a command?

"Since we are to have an understanding, Sir Charles," he said curtly at length, "let it be upon both sides. You have seen fit to give Antonia to me in marriage. You were able to compel us to a match neither of us desired, but your authority ended there. What follows concerns we two alone, and I have no intention of treating her in a manner calculated to destroy whatever small chance we have of living together in some degree of amity."

He expected this uncompromising rejoinder to throw Kelshall into an even more violent fury, but to his surprise it had the opposite effect. Sir Charles looked at him with bright, mocking eyes, and gave way to a spasm of his silent laughter.

"What, has she ensnared you already, the black-eyed witch? Have a care, St. Arvan! It was beauty such as hers which destroyed my son. It may well lead you to destruction also."

"I thank you for the warning," Geraint said shortly, "and now I will beg you to excuse me. The service you required of me I have performed. Let the matter rest there!"

"Wait!" Kelshall spoke peremptorily to check him in the act of turning away. "I have another warning to give you, and you would do well to heed it. I have very little time left to live, and from the moment of my death, you will be in mortal danger."

His voice was calm and matter-of-fact, so different from his previous tone that Geraint was impressed almost against his will. He looked searchingly at Kelshall, and the brilliant, piercing eyes, the more compelling by reason of the living death's head in which they were set, looked levelly back at him, at that moment wholly sane.

"In mortal danger," the old man repeated. "As long as I live it is in my power to bestow elsewhere the fortune my kinsman covets, but when I die it will pass to you. Should you die without issue, Antonia will have it all."

"Antonia," Geraint pointed out. "Not Roger Kelshall."

A sneer twisted Sir Charles's lips. "Roger has a son."

"Vincent!" Geraint said softly. "I had forgotten him. What you say, sir, is logical, always supposing that your kinfolk harbour such a design, but from my knowledge of Vincent Kelshall, I take leave to doubt it."

Sir Charles moved his head impatiently. "Vincent is nothing! A spineless young fool, from all accounts. It is his father you must guard against. He murdered my son and, given the opportunity, he will murder you."

"So that my widow—my very wealthy widow—may marry his son." A spark of amusement kindled in Geraint's eyes. "An ingenious scheme, but Mr. Kelshall, if indeed he cherishes such an ambition, may find it easier to plan than to accomplish."

"Do not be over-confident," Sir Charles advised him dryly. "Roger Kelshall has cunning, and the patience of the devil himself. He will wait until he learns how and where to strike with most chance of success; he'll not risk trying to remove you from his path by means of a duel, as he murdered Anthony years ago."

That, at least, was certain, Geraint reflected with a touch of grim humour. He had fought his first duel, victoriously, when he was eighteen, and since then his affairs of honour had been numerous enough to earn him the reputation of a notable duellist. Roger Kelshall must be well over fifty, and whatever his prowess at the time of Anthony Kelshall's death, he was not likely now to risk a meeting with an accomplished swordsman nearly thirty years his junior. If he did cherish any murderous design— and Geraint was not yet convinced that this was anything but a figment of Sir Charles's demented imagination—he was more likely to try to carry it out by stealth.

He walked across to the nearest window and stood looking at the wintry scene outside, the formal gardens bare and flowerless, and, beyond them, the wooded hills which enclosed the house on every side. What truth, if any, was there in Sir Charles's suspicions of his kinsman? Roger Kelshall had killed his cousin Anthony; Sir Charles, to spite him, had made Anthony's illegitimate daughter his heiress; now he had compelled Geraint to marry her. These were the facts. What else could all the rest be but a madman's fantasy?

A slight sound behind him made him turn, and he saw that a discreet-looking manservant, obviously Sir Charles's valet, had come into the room and was leaning across to murmur something in his master's ear. Kelshall listened, nodded, and dismissed the man with a gesture; then, when he had gone, summoned Geraint again to the bedside.

"You will need to be constantly on your guard, St. Arvan," he said, taking up the conversation as though there had been no interruption. "Remember that you have a wife wedded to you against her will, and if Roger Kelshall seeks to enlist her aid, she is likely to give it out of sheer malice. If she begins to speak you fair, trust her the less."

Geraint looked at him, one eyebrow mockingly raised. "You paint a charming picture of connubial bliss, Sir Charles. One calculated to sow discord between us from the first. Is it likely, though, that even to be free of me Antonia would join forces with the man who killed her father?"

"It is more than likely. It is certain," Kelshall replied grimly. "I have not been entirely frank with you on that score." He paused, regarding Geraint with bright, malevolent eyes. "You are not, I fancy, a man who takes kindly to being slighted, so I advise you to go at once to a small inn, called the Chime of Bells, which stands just beyond the park. The servants will tell you how to find it. I have just had word that your wife is on her way there—to keep an assignation with Vincent Kelshall."

In the small, wainscoted parlour of the Chime of Bells, Antonia sat on a high-backed settle before a blazing fire. Facing her, staring at her with an expression of incredulous dismay, stood a slight young man of medium height, with very regular features, and long-lashed grey eyes which lent an almost girlish appearance to his comely face. He seemed stunned by what she had just told him, and it was some moments before he found his voice to say, with a slight stammer:

"It c-cannot be true! It cannot! Even he could not do so d-dastardly a thing!"

"The fact remains that he has done it!" There was a faint note of impatience in Antonia's voice which was lost upon her companion. "I have been forced to marry this Geraint St. Arvan. I am his wife."

"His wife!" Vincent groaned, dropping on to the settle beside her and burying his face in his hands. "It is all my fault! If only I had gone back to London before Sir Charles found out that we had met! We should have been patient, waited until you came of age."

"It was not your fault, Vincent." Antonia spoke more gently now, and laid a hand on his arm. "I persuaded you to stay. You had shown me the first happiness I had ever known, and I could not bear to let you go. I did not see what my grandfather could do except disown me, and I cared nothing for that. Besides, I felt sure he would not do it." As though unable to be still, she sprang up and began to move about the room, the skirts of her crimson habit sweeping softly across the floor. "Oh, damn him to hell! Will he never die?"

"Antonia!" Vincent raised his head; his voice was shocked. "Dearest, you should not speak so. After all, he is your grandfather."

"Does that weigh with him?" she retorted passionately. "What kindness has he ever shown me? You cannot even imagine what my life has been! That great, cold house with the woods all about it, and my grandfather brooding there like some evil spider in a web, watching me with those awful eyes!" She broke off, biting her lip, and after a little continued more calmly: "Do you know what my earliest memory is? It is of being held up to look at my father's portrait, while Sir Charles made me learn by heart the story of his murder. *His* eyes, too, were of that strange, light blue, piercing but colourless. They used to watch me from the portrait as my grandfather's did in reality, until I do not know which I feared and hated most. They were watching, the painted eyes and the real, when Sir Charles told me yesterday that our secret had been betrayed. They were watching while I was married to St. Arvan."

"Poor child!" Vincent came to stand beside her, taking her hands in his. "Oh, Antonia, I wanted so much to take you away from him, to make you happy!"

Her hands were passive in his clasp; the dark eyes met his inscrutably. "I would have gone with you, Vincent, had you wished it," she said slowly, "but you would not have it so."

"It would have been wrong. For your sake I could not agree."

"For my sake?" she repeated. "Are you sure it was not for the sake of my fortune?"

"Antonia!" Pain and reproach mingled in the indignant cry. "You c-cannot believe that! I love you! I have loved you from the first moment I saw you."

"What is love?" she broke in impatiently. "You say you love me. Sir Charles loves the memory of his dead wife and son. St. Arvan loves my fortune. And I?" She shook her head. "I do not know."

"Do you not love me, Antonia?" he pleaded, but she jerked her hands free and moved away from him towards the table in the centre of the room.

"What would you have me reply to that? If I loved you to distraction it would not alter the fact that I am married to St. Arvan." She paused, moving her fingers idly across the surface of the table. "You say you know him, Vincent. What manner of man is he?"

"We have met, but I do not know him well—nor wish to! He has a wild reputation—gambling, duelling, flirting." He broke off abruptly and came across to the table. "Oh, devil take St. Arvan! Antonia, you did not mean it —about my w-wanting your fortune, I mean?"

For a moment she continued sullenly to regard him, but then her expression softened and she laid her hands on his shoulders. "No, I did not mean it," she said gently. "Forgive me."

He put his arms about her and took the kiss which was clearly offered, but timidly, because so melting a mood was rare. Though he worshipped her with slavish devotion, he was secretly a little afraid of her.

"I trust, madam," said a mocking voice behind them, "that this embrace is merely a token of cousinly good wishes on the occasion of your marriage."

Antonia and Vincent started apart and swung round, both flushing scarlet, she with anger and he with embarrassment. From the doorway, his wide shoulders propped against the side of it in a manner which suggested that he had been there for some time, Geraint was blandly regarding them.

"L-let me explain, St. Arvan!" Vincent said hastily. "You don't understand . . . !"

"Your pardon, Kelshall. I understand perfectly." Geraint sauntered into the room, tossed his hat on to the table and began to strip off his gloves. "I must point out, however, that a considerable change has recently taken place in your kinswoman's circumstances."

"Not so great a change," Antonia broke in furiously, "that it gives you the right to spy on me."

"No?" He looked at her in mock surprise, and though his face was solemn, the blue eyes were full of laughter. "I was under the impression. . . ." He paused, and, taking her left hand, thoughtfully regarded the plain gold ring on the third finger. "I knew I could not be mistaken! We were married yesterday."

She wrenched her hand free and for a moment he thought she would strike him, but instead she said, her voice unsteady with anger: "Did you have the impertinence to follow me here?"

"Naturally, m'dear," he replied lightly. "As I said, I understand perfectly. You wish to demonstrate that yesterday's ceremony means nothing whatsoever to you. Well, the point is taken, and now it is my turn to make something clear to you."

He had pulled off both gloves as he spoke and was drawing them idly through his hand, while Vincent watched him with a hint of uneasiness. Geraint observed it, and laughed.

"Be easy, Kelshall! I do not intend to dash them in your face and demand satisfaction." The gloves were pitched on top of the hat; he perched himself on the corner of the table, one booted foot swinging clear of the floor. "No, I merely wish to speak a word of warning—in

the friendliest possible spirit, I assure you. Miss Kelshall
might receive your declarations, even your embraces, with
propriety. Mrs. St. Arvan may not. Do I make myself
clear?"

"Yes, d-damn you!" Vincent was white with rage and
alarm. "You mean to come between us!"

An eyebrow shot up. "My dear Kelshall, this remark
should surely be addressed by the husband to the—er—
admirer, and not the other way about? However, you
grasp my meaning perfectly. In the circumstances, I fear I
can do nothing else."

"One moment!" Antonia, chagrined at being thus ignored, spoke sharply. "It may be that I have something to
say on that score."

"You have a deal to say, m'dear, I don't doubt, but we
need not trouble Kelshall to hear it. That would embar-
rass him, for husband and wife should never quarrel in
the presence of a third person."

With an inarticulate exclamation Vincent took a pace
towards him, his fists clenching. Geraint did not move,
and a smile still lingered about his mouth, but something
in the level blue eyes and the lazy poise of the tall figure
made Vincent think better of whatever he had intended.
He halted, looking uncertainly at Antonia.

"You had better go, Vincent," she said in answer to the
unspoken question. "Nothing can be gained by brawling
here. At present we have no choice but to part."

" 'At present'," Geraint remarked thoughtfully. "An
ambiguous phrase! However . . ." He rose to his feet,
picked up Vincent's hat, gloves and riding-whip, and put
them into his hands. "Take comfort from it, Kelshall. The
parting, it seems, is to be merely temporary." He went to
the door and opened it. "Good-day to you—cousin."

Without quite knowing how it had happened, Vincent
found himself in the tap-room, with the parlour door

closed firmly in his face. For a moment he stood undecided, then, clapping his hat on his head, strode furiously from the inn.

In the parlour Geraint, having closed the door, strolled back to his seat on the table's edge. Standing before the fire, Antonia scornfully regarded him.

"Upon my soul, you should have been an actor!" she said, her lip curling. "Last night the chivalrous hero, today the jealous husband. What part will you be playing next, I wonder?"

He drew a snuff-box from his pocket and took a pinch in a leisurely fashion. "There is one part I will never play, m'dear, and that is the cuckold. You will cease to encourage the attentions of that pretty fellow, if you value his safety."

"My question is answered," she said contemptuously. "The new role is that of duellist, of bully-swordsman, but it impresses me no more than the rest. Vincent is my cousin. If I choose to spend my time in his company, I shall do so."

"Oh, if we are to make a family matter of it . . ." He shrugged. "The bonds of kinship, however, did not prevent his father from killing yours, or the son from trying to win the same prize by more peaceful means."

Her chin went up. "That is a lie!"

He shrugged again. "As you wish, m'dear. Tell me, why did you not elope with that young spark before your grandfather learned of your meeting?" She bit her lip and her eyes faltered away from his. Geraint laughed softly. "He wouldn't, eh? I thought not."

Colour flamed into her face again. "Perhaps I refused to elope with him. There seemed no need, for I never dreamed Sir Charles would force me into this travesty of marriage. I am almost of age, and he cannot live much longer. I could afford to wait."

"Thus gaining both the fortune and the husband of your choice? Madam, you should have been named Prudence. Only Sir Charles was too wily for you and in the end you lost both—and, unless you are circumspect, may well lose Cousin Vincent altogether, for if I suspect that you have been unfaithful to me, lose him you will."

He spoke lightly, but as she met his eyes she realised that without doubt he meant what he said. The knowledge shook her confidence, but she dissembled and spoke impatiently.

"That is ridiculous! I mean nothing to you, nor you to me."

"You are my wife. The marriage was not of my seeking, but since you now bear my name, you will conduct yourself becomingly. If you do not, I promise that you will most bitterly regret it."

For a few seconds the dark eyes met and held the blue, and it was as though swords had been crossed in the quiet room. Then Antonia, trembling with anger, moved forward until she stood within a yard of him.

"Do not try me too far," she said in a low, fierce voice. "I can be a dangerous enemy, for I have been taught only too well how to hate."

Laughter leapt into his eyes again, and the brief moment of seriousness was past. "Then it is time you were taught to love," he replied, and put out a lazy hand towards her.

She evaded it and fled to the far side of the room. Surprised, for he had expected her to stand her ground and probably strike him, he followed, only to check as steel glittered suddenly in her hand.

"I warned you," she said breathlessly, "and I do not threaten idly."

"Nor I," he said with a laugh, and went on.

As he reached her she struck at him with the knife, but his hand moved just as quickly, and closed about her wrist. Beneath the ruthless pressure of his fingers her own were helpless, and with a gasp she let the weapon fall clattering to the floor. Geraint set his foot on it, then pulled her into his arms and kissed her, but not diffidently as Vincent had done. When he let her go she backed away from him to the wall and leaned there, staring at him, breathing quickly, her eyes wide in her pale face.

Geraint stooped to pick up the dagger. It was a dainty thing with a slender blade, and a hilt inlaid with gold and turquoise. Though it was obviously very old, when he tested the blade with a fingertip he found it razor-sharp, and knew that for all its lack of size it was capable of dealing a mortal blow. "A pretty toy!" he remarked. "I confess I did not expect you to be armed." He glanced up, lifting an inquiring eyebrow. "Is it your usual custom, or one assumed for my benefit?"

Now at last Antonia moved, making a determined effort to recover some of her former dignity. "That," she said, "you will never know. Now, by your leave, I will return home."

"I will escort you. You should not ride alone about the countryside."

"A few hundred yards will take me into the park," she said ungraciously, "and I prefer my own company."

He shrugged, but made no reply, and she moved towards the door. As she reached it he spoke again.

"Antonia."

For an instant she hesitated, her back towards him, then, suspiciously, she turned. He flicked the dagger on to the table, so that its point bit into the wood and it stood there quivering, its hilt gleaming dully.

"Take your trinket, madam," he said, smiling. "You may need it."

A momentary pause, and then she returned to the

table, gripped the dagger's hilt and wrenched it free. She seemed about to speak, then, changing her mind, went out without another word. Geraint was left gazing at the closed door, a reflective smile lingering about his lips.

He rode back to Kelshall Park in no very amiable frame of mind. He felt that he was being made a fool of, and the conviction had aroused a temper which was never more dangerous than when it was masked by a smile and a careless jest. Sir Charles had not been frank with him, either about the facts of Antonia's parentage or her association with Vincent Kelshall, and Geraint was beginning to wonder if anything else had been kept from him.

As soon as he reached the house he demanded another meeting with its master, only to be told that Sir Charles was occupied with his lawyer and had given explicit orders that he was not to be disturbed. After a few moments of angry deliberation, Geraint asked the whereabouts of Mr. Thornbury.

He found the chaplain, who appeared to combine the duties of secretary with that of caring for the spiritual needs of the household, busily writing at a desk in the library, but he laid aside his pen and got up when Geraint came in. There was a somewhat wary expression on his pink, chubby face.

"Good-day, Mr. St. Arvan. How may I be of service to you?"

"By giving me plain answers, Mr. Thornbury, to a number of pertinent questions," Geraint replied crisply. "I have had a surfeit, during the past twenty-four hours, of hints and veiled disclosures."

The uneasiness in Thornbury's face deepened. "What is it, sir, that you wish to know? It may not be within my power to tell you."

"Let us put that to the test." Geraint strolled forward to seat himself on the edge of the desk, motioning Thornbury to resume his place behind it. "Were you aware, for example, when you came to me in Newgate, that Antonia is acquainted—intimately acquainted—with her cousin, Vincent Kelshall?" Thornbury hesitated, and Geraint added grimly: "Perhaps I should tell you that I found them together just now at the Chime of Bells, whither Sir Charles had been obliging enough to direct me."

The chaplain's eyes lifted sharply to meet his, filled now with alarm. "What happened?"

"Nothing dramatic, I assure you." Geraint was watching him closely, the keenness of his glance belying his careless tone. "I indicated to Mr. Kelshall that I could not permit his continued attentions to my wife, and he—er—withdrew. Did you suppose I had considered myself sufficiently affronted to demand satisfaction?"

"The thought did pass through my mind, sir," Mr. Thornbury admitted apologetically. "I ask your pardon." He hesitated, and then, with an air of resolution, added abruptly: "That may, of course, have been Sir Charles's purpose in sending you there."

"What?" Geraint spoke incredulously, but a moment's consideration assured him that it might well be so. Sir Charles's son had been killed by Roger Kelshall in a duel; to the crazed old man it might seem like poetic justice to contrive a similar fate for Roger's own son.

"Sir Charles should have informed himself more particularly," he said dryly after a pause. "In spite of my numerous meetings I have never yet killed my man—nor will, without sufficient cause."

"In this instance, Mr. St. Arvan, such cause is wholly lacking," the chaplain assured him earnestly. "I can give you my word on that."

"There is no need, Mr. Thornbury. What I saw and heard at the inn persuaded me of it." A derisive smile flickered across his lips. "From what I know of Vincent Kelshall, I should be astonished if it were otherwise."

Thornbury regarded him uncertainly. "You know Mr. Vincent, sir?"

"We have a passing acquaintance, but our tastes are too dissimilar for anything more." Geraint frowned at the chaplain. "You have not yet answered my question. Did you know that he and Antonia were acquainted?"

"Yes, Mr. St. Arvan, I did. Sir Charles discovered it before I left for London. It was that discovery which finally persuaded him to agree to my suggestion that I should approach you."

Geraint's brows lifted. *"Your* suggestion, Mr. Thornbury?"

The chaplain nodded. "As I told you, sir, I had heard from my sister of the disaster which had overtaken you. I owe your family a debt of gratitude, for it was your grandfather who made it possible for me to take Holy Orders, and at last I saw an opportunity to repay it."

"At the same time serving Sir Charles's purpose. *I* am not ungrateful to you, but the old gentleman must have been desperate indeed to agree to such a scheme, and that, frankly, I cannot understand. Antonia is not only an heiress, she is extremely beautiful, and those two facts might surely have been expected to outweigh even the unfortunate circumstances of her birth when it came to finding her a husband. Or is there something more, which I do not yet know?"

"Nothing, Mr. St. Arvin, upon my word," Thornbury replied solemnly. "The difficulty arose because Sir Charles was adamant that her husband must be a man of good family. Perhaps if he had been less bitterly ashamed of her parentage, or even if he had contrived to dissemble it, the facts might have been forgotten, but he has never made any secret of his feelings, to her or to others. To him, she exists for one purpose only. To prevent Roger Kelshall from inheriting, and to ensure that the estate and fortune pass to one of Sir Charles's own blood. To a direct descendant of Anthony Kelshall. That is the obsession which has ruled his life for more than twenty years."

Geraint was frowning. "You admit, then, that Sir Charles is not wholly sane?"

"Can there be any doubt on that score, sir?" Thornbury replied with a sigh. "Oh, his mind remains clear enough where the administration of his affairs is concerned, but no man who allows himself to be so completely possessed by hatred can be entirely normal."

"Yet you appear to see nothing wrong in abetting his mad schemes," Geraint said with sudden sternness. "In my opinion, a man of your cloth should instead have been concerned to protect the girl from them."

"That has always been my endeavour, sir." Mr. Thornbury, leaning back in his chair, looked up at him with a curious dignity. "I would have left this house years ago if not for the pity and concern I felt for that unhappy child."

"Concern which expresses itself in the suggestion that she should be forced to marry a stranger! A man of whom you know little besides his name, and that little nothing to his credit! You see, sir, I cherish few illusions about myself."

"Mr. St. Arvan, I believe you do yourself less than justice," Thornbury replied seriously. "I have been desperately anxious about Miss Antonia. She knows nothing of the world outside Kelshall Park, for she has been kept here like a prisoner all her life, meeting no one except the members of this household, and her governesses and teachers." He saw the disbelief in Geraint's eyes and nodded grimly. "I do not exaggerate, sir. Her grandfather spared no expense where her education was concerned—

she has been well taught in every accomplishment expected of a lady of quality—yet never for a moment was she allowed to forget that she is here on sufferance. Watched over and guarded like the heroine of some old legend, but knowing all the while that such concern was prompted by hatred and not by affection. Can you wonder that she was determined to escape as soon as she came of age, even if it meant going alone and penniless into a world of which she has no experience whatsoever? Or that I was equally determined to prevent such a disaster?"

"Some might argue that the marriage which you helped to contrive for her is only a little less disastrous," Geraint remarked ironically. "Why in the fiend's name did you not aid her to wed young Vincent, if that is what she desired?"

"Because I do not trust him, sir, or his father. He did not meet Miss Antonia by chance. He came to this neighbourhood under an assumed name and deliberately set out to win her confidence and regard. Is that the action of an honest man?"

"Of a prudent one, perhaps, having regard to the circumstances. You are assuming that it is his ambition to possess the Kelshall fortune, but I do not think him capable of such worldliness. He is a romantic dreamer, a self-styled poet! He might well fall victim to Antonia's beauty and strange, tragic history, but a fortune-hunter? No, Mr. Thornbury, you are wide of the mark there."

"Perhaps I am, sir," the chaplain agreed equably, "but if you have judged Vincent Kelshall correctly, you may be sure that his father has done likewise. Perhaps it was at his command the boy came wooing Miss Antonia, and if it were, then Vincent is incapable of offering her the protection which I am convinced she needs."

"Protection from whom, Mr. Thornbury? From Roger Kelshall or Sir Charles?"

"From both, sir," the other man replied firmly. "From both, and from the cruel, unnatural way of life their enmity has forced upon her. Protection which you, I am sure, can give her—if you choose."

"If I choose?" Geraint repeated thoughtfully. He was silent for a little while, and Mr. Thornbury watched him anxiously, trying in vain to read the keen, reckless face. At last Geraint turned to look at him; there was an ironical expression in his eyes. "Yet you know as well as I, sir, that that choice has already been made for me. It was made at the moment Antonia became my wife."

Towards evening on the following day, Antonia was in the library when Geraint came into the room. Since their encounter at the inn she had taken pains to avoid being alone with him, and they had met only at table, in the protective presence of Mr. Thornbury and the servants. He had made no attempt to seek her company, and that he did so now awoke in her a faint uneasiness. She rose quickly from her chair with the intention of leaving.

"A moment, madam, if you please," he said courteously. "I wish to speak to you."

She frowned. "It is a wish I do not share," she retorted coldly, and swept past him to the door, but he reached it before her and barred her way with outstretched arm. He seemed amused.

"Don't run away, m'dear," he said, smiling. "I give you my word you have nothing to fear."

At that deliberate provocation she stiffened, and anger kindled in her eyes. "To fear?" she said contemptuously. "You flatter yourself, sir."

His smile broadened. "Do I? However, you have your dagger, and I am sure would not hesitate to use it."

"What do you wish to say to me?" she broke in impatiently. "If it is of any importance, I pray you say it and have done."

He bowed, his eyes glinting with laughter. "Of little importance to you, I have no doubt. I desired merely to inform you that I shall be leaving for London within the next few days."

"Leaving?" For an instant surprise drove the annoyance from her face; then she shrugged. "As you say, of little importance to me."

"True—unless you care to accompany me. You would find London, I think, more amusing than your present surroundings."

"London!" Antonia clasped her hands, her eyes shining. For a moment the hostile woman vanished, and an eager girl stood in her place, but then her face clouded again. "He will not let me go."

"Sir Charles has already given his consent—though not, I admit, until I pointed out to him that when you married me, he relinquished all authority over you." Geraint spoke pensively, but he still looked amused. "It was, I fancy, the first time that point had been brought home to him."

She looked suspiciously at him. "Why should you trouble yourself to please me?"

"To please you?" The mocking eyebrow lifted; he laughed softly. "At risk of seeming ungallant, m'dear, I must point out that I am pleasing myself. I shall go to London because I find this place intolerable. You may go with me, or, if you prefer his company to mine, you may remain with your grandfather. It is for you to choose."

The bantering tone stirred her to annoyance again. She shrugged and said indifferently: "I will think about it. Now pray have the goodness to let me pass."

He grinned, but stepped aside and opened the door for her. As she moved past him he put out his hand to grasp her right arm, for on the wrist, below the fall of fine lace in which her sleeve ended, a bruise showed dark against the white skin.

"How came you by that?" he asked abruptly.

"Need you ask?" Her voice was scornful. "Your hand set it there."

"Mine?" He frowned, remembering how he had wrested the dagger from her the previous day. "I did not mean to hurt you," he added, and dropped a kiss lightly on her wrist. "I'm sorry."

She coloured, and pulled her hand away. "It is nothing," she said shortly. "I had forgotten it."

She went quickly out of the library and up to the little parlour which was still her own private domain. Shutting the door, she walked across and stood staring at her reflection in a mirror which hung upon the wall.

"London!" she said aloud. "To escape at last from this place! I believe I will go with him." She stood thinking, fingering her right wrist until, becoming aware of the action, she flushed and made an impatient movement. "I shall most certainly go," she told her reflection with a hint of defiance. "Vincent will be in London." But her decision, as she realised with some disquiet, had been reached before any recollection of her cousin entered her head.

Part Two

At a well-known posting-house not far from London, Geraint and Antonia had halted to dine on the second day of their journey. The meal was over but, since the bitterly cold weather continued, they were both reluctant to leave the cosy parlour with its blazing fire for the discomfort of a draughty post-chaise. Antonia had moved to a seat by the hearth and was idly nibbling sweetmeats from the dish at her elbow, while Geraint, still at table, had turned his chair to face the fire and, with his fingers curled lightly round the stem of his glass, gazed thoughtfully before him in a mood of unusual abstraction.

Seeing him thus preoccupied, his wife studied him with an intentness she would otherwise have scorned to betray. Now, after a week's acquaintance, he still baffled her as much as he had at the outset. Then she had judged him to be an unscrupulous opportunist, cynically trading his ancient name for her grandfather's wealth, with no more regard for her feelings than the old man showed. He had warned her that she would not find him a complaisant husband, yet he made no demands upon her, and had even prevailed upon Sir Charles to let her go to London.

He appeared indifferent, yet could be unexpectedly perceptive. When the gates of Kelshall Park had finally swung shut behind them, Antonia had experienced a moment of sheer panic at the thought of the unknown future. She thought she was successfully hiding it, but Geraint said lightly:

"Even a prison may be regretted if it is all one has ever known, but freedom is no less desirable on that account."

"Freedom?" She had too much spirit to let that pass, even though she could not keep a betraying tremor from her voice. "I am but exchanging one prison for another."

"You misjudge me, m'dear," he murmured reproachfully. "I give you my word that you will not find me too exacting a gaoler."

She looked resentfully at him, suspecting him of mockery, but, reading only amusement in his eyes, turned her head away, with an ill-humoured shrug to mask her bewilderment. She could not understand him, this man who seemed to regard life itself as a jest, and met reproaches and contempt alike with irrepressible laughter. Nothing in her experience had prepared her for so devil-may-care an attitude, for even Vincent, taking himself and life with the utmost seriousness, had done little to lighten the gloom which had always surrounded her. Geraint appeared to take nothing seriously, not even his own part in the infamous bargain with Sir Charles.

Against her will she found herself comparing the two men. Vincent had vowed eternal devotion, sworn to rescue her from her grandfather's tyranny, yet accomplished nothing. Geraint, making no promises, yet offered her escape like a gift tossed carelessly into her lap, for her to accept or not as she chose. She did not think it would have mattered to him which decision she made.

Yet, uncaring or not, he had been unfailingly attentive during their journey. To Antonia, who had never been farther from Kelshall Park than the nearest market town,

and that only once or twice during her life, everything
was of the utmost interest—the changing aspect of the
countryside; the villages through which they passed; Ox-
ford, where they had halted for the night. Geraint willingly answered all her eager questions, even succeeding,
from time to time, in bringing a smile to her lips, so that
something approaching friendliness was established between them. On her part it was entirely passive, but her
resentment towards him was for the time being in
abeyance, and now she could even contemplate confiding
to him a dread which had been with her throughout their
journey.

She was still trying to bring herself to speak when the
tall clock in the corner uttered a throaty wheeze and then
chimed the hour with unexpected sweetness. Geraint
came out of his reverie with a start; he swallowed the rest
of his wine and got up.

"Time we were on our way if we are to reach London
tonight," he remarked, and went to pull the bell-rope.
"I'll have the horses put to."

Antonia nodded, stifling a sigh, and Geraint paused
beside her chair to look down at her.

"Tired, m'dear? Take heart, the journey will soon be
over."

She shook her head. "I am not tired. It is merely . . ."
She broke off, carefully smoothing a small crease from
her skirt, her eyes avoiding his. "Has it not occurred to
you that I may not be received in polite society?"

He frowned. "Who put that notion into your head?
Your grandfather?"

"Yes," she admitted reluctantly, "when he sent for me
just before we left yesterday. He said that I was rejoicing
too soon in my escape from him. That you were a fool to
take me to London, and when you found that no one
would receive me, because of my mother, you would soon
pack me off home again." She looked up suddenly with a

hint of defiance. "Do not misunderstand me! It is the
Kelshall blood in me that I hate and despise, and not the
gipsy, but it may be that Sir Charles is right."

"You will be received," Geraint said reassuringly. "Do
you not see, my dear girl, that Sir Charles's only object in
saying such a thing was to distress you? He will not disclose the facts, for his own pride's sake, and for the same
reason, Roger Kelshall is unlikely to do so. You have
lived so retired that you have no acquaintances in London, but I have many, and as my wife you will be accepted without question. Set your mind at rest on that."

She looked doubtful. "Suppose the circumstances of
our marriage become known?"

"Why should they, any more than the facts of your
parentage? There will be speculation, of course, but it will
last only until a fresh cause for gossip is discovered—
which is to say a week at most.

"Are you sure?" Her eyes anxiously searched his face.
"Much as I hate my grandfather's house, I would rather
go back there at once than risk such humiliation."

He leaned forward, resting one hand on the back of her
chair and laying the other over hers, now clasped tightly
together in her lap. "I am sure," he said quietly. "Believe
me, I would not take you to London if there were any
chance that you would be either made unhappy or humiliated by your reception there."

Antonia made no attempt to withdraw her hands. Her
lips were parted, and her eyes, still raised to his, held a
wondering look, softer than any he had yet seen in them.
Then, before either of them could speak again, the door
opened to admit a depressed-looking servant, his long
nose pink-tipped with cold.

"What the devil do you want?" Geraint straightened up
quickly and directed towards the intruder a look of such
fury that the unfortunate man instinctively recoiled. He

moistened his lips, and opened and closed them several times before any sound emerged.

"You—you rang, sir," he muttered at last.

"What? Oh, yes! Have my horses put to—and don't stand there gaping, confound you! Get out, and see to it."

The servant retreated in some disorder towards the door, which he had neglected to close completely. For this reason, Geraint's imperative tones had floated out into the passage, to reach the ears of a lady who had just descended the stairs.

She halted abruptly at the sound of his voice, staring wide-eyed in the direction from which it had come. Then with a stifled exclamation she ran forward to the door of the parlour, almost colliding with the servant, who stepped hastily aside to let her pass. The occupants of the room did not at once perceive her, for Antonia, with heightened colour, was staring fixedly at the fire, and Geraint watching her with a faint frown. The newcomer, pausing in the doorway, had eyes only for him.

"Geraint!" she said breathlessly.

He started violently and swung round. Framed in the doorway was a charming picture, all in shades of blue. A silk hood, tied over unpowdered curls of palest gold, framed a face of cameo-like perfection; a velvet cloak, ermine-trimmed, shrouded a figure whose dainty proportions were those of a Dresden shepherdess; china-blue eyes, framed by long lashes, regarded him incredulously. For a moment she remained poised there, like a bird halted in mid-flight, then, casting aside a large ermine muff, fluttered forward with outstretched hands.

"Geraint!" she repeated. "It is indeed you! When I heard your voice, I thought I must be dreaming! What miracle brings you here?"

Geraint, who upon catching sight of her had uttered what sounded to Antonia suspiciously like a smothered oath, recovered himself and bowed very formally, ignoring the proffered hands. His wife was not surprised by this forbearance. The young lady, she judged, needed very little encouragement to cast herself into his arms.

"This is an unexpected pleasure, Miss Chalgrove," he said repressively. "I trust I see you in good health?"

Miss Chalgrove's hands dropped to her sides and she looked up at him in hurt bewilderment, her lower lip trembling. Before she could speak again Geraint turned to Antonia, thus making the other girl fully aware of her presence.

"Madam," he continued, "give me leave to present Miss Jessica Chalgrove."

Antonia's cold appraisal had informed her that though the young lady was dressed far more modishly than herself, she was of quite diminutive stature. She rose gracefully to her own stately height and curtsied with the condescension of a queen, while Geraint, with something less than his usual easy assurance, completed the introduction.

"Miss Chalgrove—my wife."

The vision in blue had begun, somewhat suspiciously, to return Antonia's curtsy, but that announcement turned it into what was probably the least graceful reverence of her life. Straightening up, she stood looking from one to the other in stricken dismay.

"Your wife?" she whispered. "Oh, Geraint, no!"

It was a cry straight from the heart, but a moment later she had recovered her composure. A mask of polite interest veiled the despair which for a brief instant had shown in her face, and she even achieved a smile.

"Why then, I must wish you happy," she said. "I am delighted to make your acquaintance, ma'am. You must forgive the informality I used in walking in upon you." The smile became faintly malicious. "Geraint and I are very old friends."

"There is no need to apologise, Miss Chalgrove," Antonia replied, in a voice of such honeyed sweetness that Geraint glanced uneasily at her. "You thought my husband was alone. I realise that you would not have entered had you been aware of *my* presence."

Miss Chalgrove's eyes narrowed, and her small figure stiffened beneath the enveloping cloak, but before she could think of a fitting retort a small, plump lady, opulently dressed in russet-coloured velvet and sables, swept into the room, saying in tones of deep displeasure:

"Jessica, are you lost to all sense of what is fitting? To wander alone about an inn, and thrust yourself into a private room occupied by a gentleman—upon my soul! I think you have lost your wits! As for you, St. Arvan, I am astonished . . . !"

"Mama!" Jessica interrupted in a constrained voice. "I think you have not perceived this lady. It is Mrs. St. Arvan."

The indignant woman, checked in the full flight of her denunciation, gasped and stared. She became aware that the dark stranger was curtsying to her, and dazedly acknowledged the greeting; then, groping among her furs, produced a gold-mounted lorgnette in order to study her more carefully. As she took in the full power of Antonia's striking beauty, the disbelief in her face became more pronounced.

"Mrs. St. Arvan?" she repeated, and looked suspiciously at Geraint. "Your marriage, sir, must have been a very sudden event. We have heard no whisper of it in Town."

"We were married quietly at my wife's home a week ago," he explained briefly. "Her grandfather, Sir Charles Kelshall, particularly wished it so, since his health confines him to his room."

"Kelshall?" Mrs. Chalgrove was passing from astonishment to astonishment. She looked again at Antonia. "Is it possible, ma'am, that you are related by marriage to my very old friend, Mrs. Roger Kelshall?"

"Her husband is my kinsman, ma'am," Antonia replied politely, "though I have never met him. This will be my first visit to London."

Mrs. Chalgrove let her lorgnette drop to the length of its ribbon. The familiar name of Kelshall had convinced her that Geraint was not lying, and her own observant gaze informed her that though the bride's gown sadly lacked style, its material was of the finest quality, and the cloak cast carelessly across a chair richly lined with fur, while St. Arvan's elegant attire hinted at no small degree of affluence. It suited Mrs. Chalgrove very well to find that Geraint St. Arvan had mysteriously acquired a beautiful and obviously wealthy wife, and an expression of the utmost benevolence descended upon her face.

"You must permit me to offer my felicitations, my dear," she said graciously. "To you also, sir. No doubt we shall have the pleasure of seeing you both in Town. Now we must bid you goodbye, for it grows late and I do not care to be travelling after dark. Come, Jessica."

Farewells were said, and mother and daughter went out, but in the doorway Jessica paused to look back. Anger, pain and reproach were in her face as she looked at Geraint, and then her mother called sharply to her, and she turned and passed out of sight.

Within the parlour there was silence for a moment. A cold draught swept in from the passage, making the fire smoke, and Geraint went across and shut the door. Turning back to Antonia, he said lightly:

"You see, m'dear, how groundless your fears prove to be. Mrs. Chalgrove moves in the first rank of society, and after her first surprise she accepted you without question. If you can satisfy a gimlet-eyed dowager such as she, you need have no qualms at all."

"Do you know Mrs. Chalgrove well?" Antonia asked meekly.

He shrugged. "I have met her many times. As far as a man of my generation is likely to know a lady of hers, I suppose one could say I know her tolerably well."

"And her daughter? Your acquaintaince with *her, I* fancy, is more than tolerable."

"Much more! I would go so far as to say I have found it delightful." Geraint strolled back to where she stood rigidly before the fire, and smiled down into her affronted eyes. "As delightful as I'll wager you found *your* acquaintaince with young Vincent."

"That, sir," she said angrily, "is no concern of yours."

"Precisely," he murmured. "How could it be, when at that time you and I had not even met?"

The rebuke, for all its pleasantness, was unmistakable. She flushed, and turned away to pick up her cloak, and when he took it from her and placed it about her shoulders she barely acknowledged the courtesy. In sullen silence she waited while he paid the reckoning, and then accompanied him out to the chaise.

The encounter with Jessica Chalgrove had recalled most forcibly what Vincent had told her of Geraint's reputation, which during the past twenty-four hours had faded to the back of Antonia's mind. Almost against her will, her antagonism towards her husband had been lessening, until she had even begun to enjoy his company, but Miss Chalgrove had provided a timely reminder that the lazy good humour, and the charm which had nearly convinced Antonia that his concern for her was real, were no more than the weapons of a practised flirt, deliberately and cynically used to win the hearts of credulous females.

It was a reflection which made her as angry with herself as with him.

Her mood of sullen hostility lasted for the rest of the journey, spoiling even the excitement of arriving in London and dulling her interest in the unfamiliar sights and sounds of a great city. At the busy posting-house which was their immediate destination Geraint bespoke a private parlour, a room for himself and one for Antonia and her maid, Turner, who had accompanied them in a second vehicle with the luggage.

The inn was a bewildering hurly-burly of constant comings and goings, guests arriving and departing, and servants scurrying to and fro, so that Antonia's head spun, and she could only be thankful that Geraint knew how to command attention, for she felt that, left to themselves, she and Turner would have been trampled underfoot. In what semed to her a miraculously short space of time their rooms had been prepared, the baggage carried up, and a light supper laid out in the parlour. She sat down to it without enthusiasm, and as soon as the meal was over retreated to her bedchamber.

The two days of unaccustomed travelling had made her very tired, but it was hours before she fell asleep. To one used all her life to country quietness, it seemed that London never slept, and the night was half gone before she fell into an exhausted slumber. As a result, she was very late in rising, and when she entered the parlour she found there a note from Geraint informing her that he had gone to see his lawyer about some urgent matters of business, but when these had been concluded he would be at her disposal.

Antonia ate her solitary breakfast and then went to sit by the window, watching the busy scene outside. She found it endlessly entertaining, seen from the comfortable security of the inn, but had honesty enough to realise that it would have presented a very different aspect had she been alone and unprotected in this vast, uncaring city. For the first time she admitted to herself how wildly impractical had been her original intention of leaving Kelshall Park to fend for herself as soon as she came of age; it was no wonder Geraint had laughed when she told him of it.

From this reflection, others were born. The meeting with Mrs. Chalgrove and her daughter proved him right about his wife's reception in London, and indicated, too, that for the present at least he was prepared to behave as though there were nothing unusual about their marriage, but would he continue to do so if she continually abused and flouted him? Antonia thought not; she believed that he was far less easy-going than he pretended. She had inherited a good deal of the Kelshall shrewdness even though it was frequently overwhelmed by the fiercer passions of her gipsy ancestry, and she realised that until she was firmly established in fashionable society it would be prudent to adopt a more conciliatory manner.

So when Geraint returned, a little after noon, she greeted him civilly, assured him that she had not been in the least bored during his absence, and inquired if his business with the lawyer had been satisfactorily concluded. He regarded her quizzically for a moment, but made no comment on the change in her attitude towards him.

"I trust so. I have told him that I wish to acquire, with as little delay as possible, a house in a good part of town, but as that is something which cannot be accomplished overnight, he is going to look about for a tolerable lodging where we may live meanwhile. You will not wish to remain in this place more than a day or two."

"I would prefer somewhere a little quieter," she admitted, adding with a glimmer of a smile: "Turner will be deeply thankful, I know. She is convinced that while we remain here we are likely to be robbed or murdered at any moment."

He laughed. "Assure your abigail that murder in an inn of this quality is almost unknown, and that the only robbery we are likely to suffer will be in the reckoning. Now, m'dear, I have neglected you long enough. Is there anything in particular you wish to see or to do?"

Antonia, with whom the memory of Jessica Chalgrove's exquisitely fashionable attire still rankled, answered this query without hesitation.

"Yes. I would like to buy some new clothes." Then a doubtful look came into her face. "But perhaps you do not know where . . . ?"

"I assure you that I do," he said with some amusement. "Deplorable as it may seem to you, I have considerable experience in such matters, and can undertake to convey you to the most modish establishments in London."

She looked suspiciously at him, but before she could make any comment the door was opened by one of the inn servants, who, eyeing Geraint with increased respect, announced importantly:

"My lord and my lady Mountworth to see you, Mr. St. Arvan."

Geraint uttered an exclamation of astonishment, and turned quickly as a lady and gentleman of about his own age came into the room. Lady Mountworth, a slim brunette remarkable more for vivacity and stylishness than for beauty, ran forward to catch his hand in both her own.

"Geraint, you provoking creature!" she greeted him merrily. "What a fright you have given us!"

"Lucy, by all that's wonderful!" Geraint kissed her fingers and then extended a hand to her husband. "Peter! What in the world brings you back from Italy?"

"What should bring us back but the news that you were in difficulties?" Mountworth replied with a smile, gripping the outstretched hand. "By all accounts, however, we might have spared our pains. We are to congratulate you, it seems."

"That is so!" Geraint turned to Antonia, who had risen to her feet and was regarding the newcomers in bewilderment. He took her hand and drew her into the group. "Lucy, let me present my wife."

Antonia began to curtsy, but her ladyship, it seemed, had no intention of standing on ceremony. Antonia's hands were caught in a warm clasp, and Lucy said gaily:

"Oh, do not let us be formal, for I have known Geraint all my life and I am sure that you and I are going to be great friends. What a good thing we came back to London!"

Antonia murmured some civility, and Geraint presented Lord Mountworth. Lucy, her head on one side like a bright-eyed robin, studied the younger girl with frank admiration.

"My dear, you will set a new fashion, and we brunettes shall be in the mode again. That is delightful! Simpering blondes like Jessica Chalgrove have been the rage for far too long." She caught her husband's resigned and reproving glance and clapped a hand to her mouth. "Oh, my unlucky tongue! Why do I always speak without thinking?"

No one attempted to answer this question, but Geraint said lightly:

"Am I to understand that you abandoned your tour of Italy and hurried back to England to rescue me from Newgate?"

"Of course," Lucy replied. "The news took an unconscionable time to reach us, but as soon as it did we set out for home, for surely you did not think we should leave you in that horrible prison? My dear, was it very dreadful?"

He grinned affectionately down at her. "No worse,

probably, than I deserved for being such a confounded fool. Besides," the laughing glance shifted to Antonia's face, "even a stay in Newgate can bring unexpected good fortune."

Lucy opened her lips to speak, but before she could ask the question, probably indiscreet, which was obviously in her mind, Peter said hastily:

"When we arrived in London we found that someone had been before us. You had been released, but no one knew where you were. Then this morning I chanced to meet young Chalgrove, who told me of his mother's meeting with you yesterday. I sent to the inns where you were most likely to be staying, and," he smiled and shrugged, "here we are."

"And most happy to find you," her ladyship added earnestly, "even though we come too late to be of help."

Geraint took her hand and raised it to his lips. "Dear Lucy," he said gently, "for your concern for me I am most truly grateful to you both, more grateful than words can say." He paused, and then added more lightly: "And you, at least, are not too late to be of help. This is Antonia's first visit to London and her most urgent wish is to replenish her wardrobe. In that, I am sure, she could wish for no better guide."

"That will be delightful!" Lucy exclaimed, and turned impulsively to Antonia. "My dear Mrs. St. Arvan, let us go at once. Only yesterday I saw some brocade which would suit you admirably . . . !"

"One moment, my love," Mountworth broke in with some amusement. "Geraint, do you make a long stay in London?"

Geraint replied that that was their intention, and explained the arrangements he had made. Lucy said roundly:

"How absurd! You must stay with us until you are able to set up a suitable establishment of your own."

"I quite agree," her husband added promptly. "In fact, it is only because you believed us to be still abroad that we forgive you for not coming to us in the first place."

"You are, as always, more than generous," Geraint said gratefully. "We accept your invitation with pleasure, do we not, m'dear?"

Antonia agreed. It would have been difficult to do otherwise, but in this case she had no wish to quarrel with his decision. In spite of his reassurances she had been unable to conquer all her misgivings, and felt that it would be comforting to have Lady Mountworth's support during her first days in London.

The story, recounted by Mrs. Chalgrove, of Geraint St. Arvan's astounding reappearance accompanied by a rich and beautiful bride spread rapidly through fashionable society, losing nothing in the telling. Speculation ran riot, but though there were some older people who remembered the fatal duel between Anthony and Roger Kelshall, neither man had at that time moved in the more fashionable circles, and it occurred to no one to query Antonia's antecedents. The name of Kelshall was now familiar enough, and when it became known that young Mrs. St. Arvan was the grand-daughter and heiress of the wealthy, titled head of that family, no one inquired any further. All curiosity was centred upon the means by which Geraint, incarcerated in Newgate, had accomplished so successful a match.

It was a curiosity which had to remain unsatisfied. Apart from Vincent Kelshall—and, presumably, his father—the only people in London who knew the whole story were Lord and Lady Mountworth. Antonia had accepted without protest Geraint's decision to tell them.

They were his two oldest friends, for his family and Lucy's had been neighbours, while his friendship with Peter dated from their schooldays, and since Antonia liked them both she would have been reluctant to stay in their house under false pretences.

The news that the St. Arvans were the guests of Lord Mountworth prompted a large number of ladies and gentlemen to pay a morning call at his lordship's house in Grosvenor Square. Lucy, who knew her world, warned Antonia that this was likely to happen, and said pointedly to Geraint that she trusted he would be present also.

"My dear Lucy, I would not absent myself for the world! It is not everyone who is given an opportunity to observe himself becoming one of the most envied men in London."

She chuckled appreciatively. "It is not everyone who can turn so neat a compliment, either," she retorted, "though in this instance it is no more than the simple truth. Antonia is bound to create a sensation."

Antonia, happening to catch Geraint's glance, was furious to find herself blushing. Since the Mountworths knew the truth about the marriage, why did he persist in behaving in their presence as though it had not been entered upon with the utmost reluctance on either side; and why should she be fool enough to be gratified by his practised gallantry?

Lucy's judgment proved to be sound. There was a constant stream of visitors, until Antonia's head swam with the effort of remembering names and titles, for in the space of two hours she had met more people than in the whole of her life. Lucy was delighted, and said so when, during a momentary lull, the four of them found themselves alone.

"Quite so, Lucy, but there is one thing which disappoints me." Geraint spoke so lightly that it was impossible to tell whether or not he were serious. "A familiar face is absent, though one would expect her cousin to be among the first to welcome Antonia to London. Can it be, I wonder, that he is waiting for some less public occasion?"

The door opened, and as though to give him the lie, Mr. Kelshall was announced. Antonia flashed a triumphant glance at Geraint, but to her dismay the man who entered was a stranger to her. Tall and elegant, carrying his fifty-odd years lightly, Roger Kelshall advanced to greet her ladyship.

"So!" Geraint, standing beside his wife's chair, spoke in a voice which reached her ears alone. "The arch-villain himself! You rejoiced too soon, m'dear."

She cast him a look of acute distaste, but Kelshall had turned towards her and she had no opportunity to reply. She looked up at him and her heart lurched unpleasantly, for from a thin, arrogant face, eyes of a familiar, piercing blue were steadily regarding her.

"Mrs. St. Arvan! My dear child!" Kelshall's voice was a nice blend of formality and warmth. "This is a pleasure I have long desired."

Antonia held out her hand. "I am happy to make your acquaintance, sir," she replied, but her voice was unsteady, for she could not immediately recover from the shock of those eyes so like her grandfather's. "May I present my husband?"

"Ah, yes! Your husband." Kelshall turned to Geraint, who bowed gravely enough, though a glimmer of mocking laughter danced in his eyes. "Well, St. Arvan, you are to be congratulated! The past few months have seen some extraordinary changes in your fortunes."

The vivid eyes met his squarely. "That is very true, Mr. Kelshall, but no doubt you have observed that fortune is confoundedly unpredictable. When we look for nothing, she showers favours upon us; when we expect much, we frequently receive—nothing!"

Roger's eyes narrowed, and he tapped his quizzing-glass thoughtfully against his chin. "Precisely, sir," he said softly at length. "One's luck can change from good to ill in the twinkling of an eye. It is a reflection which cannot fail to give pause to a thoughtful man."

Geraint's brows lifted. "From good to ill?" he repeated. "You are not very complimentary to your kinswoman, sir. We were discussing my fortunes, were we not?"

The elder man smiled. "Of course," he said smoothly. "A slip of the tongue, for which I ask your pardon." He turned to Antonia. "Madam, my wife desires me to present her compliments. She is indisposed, and so was unable to accompany me."

"I am sorry to hear it, sir. I trust her indisposition is not serious?"

"A slight cold, that is all. She is receiving callers, but I felt it unwise for her to venture out in this inclement weather, even for the pleasure of welcoming a kinswoman to London."

Antonia glanced sidelong at Geraint, and decided upon a gesture of defiance. "If Mrs. Kelshall is receiving visitors, sir, perhaps I may be permitted to call upon her tomorrow? I should like so much to make her acquaintance."

"My dear Mrs. St. Arvan, nothing could give her greater pleasure. It has always been a source of regret to both of us that the unhappy events of the past have prevented all communication between our families."

She raised her dark gaze to his. "The past is dead, Mr. Kelshall, and should be forgotten. I bear you no grudge, as I believe you know, and I should count myself fortunate in your friendship."

She put out her hand to him as she spoke, and he took it in both of his, patting it in a fatherly manner.

"It makes me very happy, my dear child, to hear you say so. It has troubled me to know that the hatred your grandfather bears me—naturally enough, I suppose, though no one regrets the past more bitterly than I—was being instilled also into you. The original quarrel was not of my family's seeking."

"That, sir, I can well believe. My grandfather quarrels with everyone."

"Then the resulting unhappy state of affairs is for us to remedy, my dear cousin. I will tell my wife you will wait upon her tomorrow, and now I must take my leave." He kissed her hand and turned to Lucy. "Your ladyship, permit me to bid you goodbye. I look forward to our next meeting. Gentlemen, your servant."

He went out. Geraint, leaning on the back of a chair, offered his snuff-box to Peter.

"Such scenes of family affection are extremely edifying," he remarked. "They are also, I suspect, extremely rare."

"Cynic!" Peter retorted with a grin. "If *you* quarrel with your relatives, it does not follow that everyone does likewise."

"My dear fellow, I don't quarrel with my relatives. I no longer have any."

Mountworth's brows lifted. "I thought there was an aged great-uncle at Barnet?"

"A connection by marriage only. He and my grandfather were step-brothers. I have not seen him for nearly a year. We only meet, you know, when from time to time he imagines that he is dying, and summons me to his presence. Otherwise we take care not to impose on one another."

"That," retorted Lucy, "is quite untrue. I believe you are sincerely attached to him."

Geraint laughed and shrugged. "I will own to a kindness for the old gentleman," he admitted, and turned to Antonia. "I must take you to call upon him, m'dear. That will restore me to his favour, for he has been telling me for years that I should marry."

She made no reply, but Peter, regarding his friend with some amusement, inquired: "Expectations, Geraint?"

"Gad, no! The old gentleman could well be a St. Arvan, for he squandered his substance on pleasure long ago. The truth is . . ."

"The truth is," Lucy interrupted, laughing, "that you dislike being at odds with him, and look to Antonia to set matters right. Come, confess it!"

"I fancy your ladyship is mistaken," Antonia said ungraciously. "I see no reason to suppose that I should be able to make the peace between them, so it does not seem likely that any useful purpose could be served by such a visit."

"Come, m'dear, this is ungenerous," Geraint said lightly. "If I am to bear with your family connections, you must at least be civil to mine."

She looked up at him, her eyes flashing. "I understand," she said contemptuously. "That is a threat, is it not, but perhaps you can recall the answer I made the first time you used it?"

She rose to her feet with a rustle of stiff silks and swept disdainfully from the room. Mountworth became intent upon removing an entirely imaginary speck of dust from his sleeve, while his wife, after one speaking glance at Geraint, pressed her lips firmly together with the air of one determined not to give voice to her thoughts.

He grinned unrepentantly. "Deliberate provocation, was it not? None the less, she will come with me to visit the old gentleman when the weather improves."

On the day after Roger Kelshall's visit, Antonia paid her promised call on his wife. Mrs. Kelshall, who received her warmly, was considerably younger than her husband, a handsome woman with a decided air of fashion, while the size and style of the house seemed to confirm the absurdity of Sir Charles's suspicions. Mr. Kelshall was obviously a man of substance.

For a time the two ladies made polite conversation, but presently Vincent arrived and a few minutes later Mrs. Kelshall made an excuse to leave them. Antonia wondered fleetingly who had planned this tête-à-tête, and decided regretfully that it was unlikely to have been Vincent himself.

As soon as the door had closed behind his step-mother, Vincent moved quickly to Antonia's side, sitting down beside her on the sofa and taking her hands in his.

"This is more than I dared to hope for," he said eagerly. "How did you persuade Sir Charles to let you come to London?"

"It was St. Arvan who persuaded him, not I."

"Oh," Vincent frowned. "With what purpose, I wonder?"

Something in his tone irritated her; she said with a shrug: "Do you imagine that I cared why? At last I was offered the opportunity to escape from that prison, and as yet I have found no cause to regret that I took it."

He looked at her with quick suspicion. "I still do not understand how Sir Charles was prevailed upon to let you go."

"He had little choice. It seems he had overlooked the fact that when I married, his authority over me passed to my husband."

Suspicion deepened into jealousy. He got up and went to stand by the fire. "An authority which you appear to find less irksome than that of your grandfather," he said in a hurt tone. "Perhaps by now you prefer St. Arvan's company to mine—or is it that you simply wanted to escape, and cared little who provided the means?" He took a pace towards her again. "Is it, Antonia? Is that why you said you would m-marry me?"

She did not reply at once. Before her wedding she would have answered with complete conviction that she had promised to marry him because she loved him. Now she was less certain. If her feeling for Vincent were deep and true, would she think so frequently of Geraint, or feel the need to make a conscious effort to keep her antagonism towards him alive?

"I am answered!" Vincent said dramatically after a moment. "I was a fool to imagine you l-loved me!" He dropped into a chair and took his head in his hands. "If only I had eloped with you when I had the chance! If only Sir Charles had not found out about us!"

Still she said nothing, but the dark eyes studied him with growing impatience, and an unwelcome question took shape in her mind. Had the position been reversed, would Geraint spend his time railing against fortune, or lay the blame for the situation on somebody else? Vincent's lack of spirit, and the persistence with which the thought of Geraint recurred in her mind, combined to annoy her, and where she would once have sought to comfort and encourage her cousin, she now felt more inclined to shake him.

"This is all to no purpose," she said at last, and not all her efforts could entirely keep a note of sharpness from her voice. "We may not have another opportunity to be private, and indeed, would be imprudent to create one. St. Arvan warned me that day at the inn, and I do not want to place you in danger."

"Warned you?" Vincent looked up sharply, his face rather pale. "What do you m-mean?"

Her brows lifted. "Must I be plainer? He said that if he suspected us of betraying him, he would kill you—and he meant it, no doubt of that. I am his wife, and his pride will permit no breath of scandal to touch my name."

Vincent sneered. "Does he still lay claim to pride after

his bargain with Sir Charles? Men of his stamp are all the same! Because they can handle a sword better or shoot straighter than most, they think they can browbeat any-one while their own lives remain a scandal none dare crit-icise. Oh, it is a fine husband your grandfather chose for you!"

"It is a man, at least!" she flashed, and an instant later was stricken with remorse for the words which, it seemed, had issued of their own volition from her lips. "Vincent, forgive me! I do not know what I am saying!"

"What you are th-thinking is clear enough," he said bitterly, "though I suppose I ought not be surprised. St. Arvan, they say, has a way with women." He laughed, without amusement but with a good deal of malice. "A case, no doubt, of practise bringing p-perfection!"

Antonia rose abruptly to her feet and went across to the window, making a determined effort to control her temper.

"I do not want to quarrel with you, Vincent," she said over her shoulder, "but this conversation shows how little we gain by meeting thus. What passed between us in Gloucestershire belongs to the past. I am married to St. Arvan now, and I will not give him reason for calling you out. In future we must meet only as chance directs."

"Better not to meet at all," he replied wretchedly. "If you knew how I suffer, Antonia! How the thought of you bound to that p-profligate torments me day and night!" He came across to her and possessed himself once more of her hands. "If I have spoken cruelly to you, it is be-cause of my own p-pain. You must forgive me!"

"Of course I forgive you, Vincent," she said gently, "but it does not alter my determination." She leaned for-ward and kissed his cheek. "Goodbye, my dear. For your own sake, you must try to forget."

"I shall n-never forget," he vowed, but he made no further protest against their parting. Although he was quite convinced that his heart was broken, he had no desire to expose the fragments to St. Arvan's deadly sword.

In the weeks which followed, Antonia found herself entering a world which she had scarcely known existed, a carefree world of wealth and elegance where pleasure was the constant aim. The Mountworths were acknowledged leaders of fashion, and under her ladyship's patronage young Mrs. St. Arvan was welcomed everywhere. From the old-fashioned, cheerless routine of Kelshall Park she was flung into a frivolous round of social activity, until between card-parties, balls, visits to the theatre and other fashionable diversions, she felt that she scarcely had time to catch her breath.

At first she was bewildered by it all, and agonisingly unsure of herself, but though her upbringing made casual social contacts difficult for her, it had at least taught her self-command, so that she was able to hide her fears and uncertainties. The air of aloofness this lent her, coupled with her dark, dramatic beauty, was novel enough to attract attention and before long, to her astonishment, she found that she had set a new fashion. An air of mystery was suddenly the mode.

During those first difficult days, Lucy Mountworth proved to be a good friend. Older than Antonia, and well aware of the malicious undercurrents flowing just beneath the ceremonious surface of polite society, she made of herself an unobtrusive shield between the other girl and the spite her wealth and beauty provoked in some quarters. Those ladies, foremost among them Jessica Chalgrove, who tried to patronise Geraint St. Arvan's country-bred pride, found their barbed shafts turned smilingly aside and often manipulated with such skill that they stung those who had launched them, for Lucy's seemingly inconsequential chatter was in no way a reflection of an empty head.

Yet if it was Lucy who stood between Antonia and this honeyed malice, it was Geraint who protected her from unwelcome gallantry. Inevitably, she acquired admirers. It was the fashion for gentlemen to pay court to any acknowledged beauty, to bestow upon her flowers and compliments and to compete for the privilege of performing such small services as handing her into her coach. Frequently these courtesies were a cloak for a more intimate relationship, but where Antonia was concerned the gallants, mindful of her husband's dangerous reputation, behaved with circumspection. Not that St. Arvan appeared in any way possessive—as often as not he was conducting a flirtation on his own account—but his wife's admirers soon learned that any attempt to overstep the bounds of propriety would bring him unhurriedly to her side, smiling with a lazy good humour which somehow succeeded in conveying a warning even to the most dull-witted.

Antonia herself was scarcely aware of his constant watchfulness; what she did notice was the frequency with which he seemed to be in Miss Chalgrove's company. Others noticed this, too, just as they perceived Jessica's unconcealed dislike of Mrs. St. Arvan, and the two facts together proved a fruitful source of gossip and conjecture. The whispers reached Antonia's ears and led her eventually to question Lucy.

Her ladyship looked embarrassed. "My dear, it is nothing of the least consequence. There is not the smallest need for you to disturb yourself over it."

"I am not in the least disturbed," Antonia replied calmly, "but I am constantly hearing Miss Chalgrove's name coupled in a knowing way with St. Arvan's, and I would prefer to be as well informed as everyone else appears to be."

"Well," Lucy said reluctantly, "I'll not deny that at one

time there was considerable speculation. Jessica caused
quite a stir when she first came to Town last season, for
one cannot deny that she is a pretty creature. Geraint
paid her a great deal of attention, though I shall always
maintain—and Mountworth agrees with me—that he was
prompted as much by devilment as anything else. You
see, her other most persistent suitor, and the one favoured
by her mother, is Dereham, with whom Geraint had no
patience at all."

Antonia had no difficulty in believing this. She had met
the Earl of Dereham, a humourless and somewhat bigoted
young man who looked with scorn upon the extravagant
follies of his contemporaries, and was given to moralising
about them with a solemnity of a man twice his age. Antonia had thought him a bore, and could well imagine the
effect he must have on Geraint.

"There would have been not the least harm in it," Lucy
went on, "had the silly child not taken it into her head
that Geraint was serious in his attentions. How she can
have believed such a thing I cannot imagine, for everyone
knows that he . . ."

"That he cannot resist flirting with every pretty woman
he meets," Antonia put it dryly as her friend hesitated.
"Pray, Lucy, do not try to spare my feelings. I cannot
imagine why you should think it necessary to do so."

Lucy started to say something, thought better of it for
once in her life, and instead went on: "Heaven knows,
Jessica had warnings enough—I even dropped a word in
her ear myself—but she would pay no heed. Perhaps she
thought she could change him, for she is as foolish as she
is pretty, and vain into the bargain. When we left for Italy
she was still stubbornly refusing to have anything to do
with Dereham, and poor Mrs. Chalgrove was at her wit's
end. She was terrified, you see, that Geraint would elope
with Jessica."

Antonia frowned. "I do not see why, if, as you say, no

one but Miss Chalgrove herself believed that his intentions were serious."

"Oh, Mrs. Chalgrove did not fear that his affections were engaged. She was anxious on quite another score. Jessica is an heiress in her own right, for someone—her godfather, I think it was—willed his whole fortune to her, unconditionally, upon her marriage, and everyone knew that Geraint's affairs were in a shocking muddle. Mrs. Chalgrove would give anything to see Jessica safely married to Dereham, for besides being a brilliant match, no one could even suspect him of being a fortune-hunter."

"While no one, I imagine, had any difficulty in believing it of St. Arvan?"

"Only those with too little sense or too much malice," Lucy replied with unaccustomed sharpness. "Had it been Geraint's purpose to mend his fortunes with a marriage-ring he could have done so without the least difficulty, since that silly child was throwing herself at his head in the most shameless manner. As she continues to do even now! If you have failed to observe that, my dear Antonia, you must be the only person in London who has not remarked it."

"I have observed that they are frequently in each other's company," Antonia said dryly. "What I have not detected is any sign of reluctance on St. Arvan's part."

Lucy was silent for a moment, and then she said in a reflective tone: "I have been closely acquainted with Geraint since I was three years old, and I know him as well as I know my own brothers. It is not his way to wear his heart on his sleeve. While he continues to flirt openly with Jessica—or any other woman—then believe me, my dear, his wife need have no cause for uneasiness."

Geraint's man of business had found for his client a pleasant house in Brook Street. Geraint, taking Antonia to look at it, pronounced it tolerable, and she, scorning to show any greater enthusiasm, agreed that it would do very well. Secretly she was delighted with it. The thought of a home of her own, a house where she would be mistress instead of an intruder despised and resented, filled her with an excitement she had difficulty in dissembling, and she waited in a state of painful anxiety until Geraint had told the lawyer to complete the arrangements.

As soon as this had been done she flung herself into the business of home-making. No detail was too trivial for her attention, and she gave as much thought to the choice of ornaments as to the question of furniture and hangings and the hiring of servants. She had more or less a free hand, for Geraint soon became bored with such domestic matters, but Lucy's advice was sought and readily given on many points. This was another source of pleasure to Antonia; for the first time in her life she had a woman friend of her own generation.

When at last the house was ready, and she and Geraint took possession, she waited with secret anxiety to learn if he approved of all she had done. Whatever their personal differences, she had no quarrel with his judgment of such matters, or his knowledge of what the fashionable world would or would not consider correct. There were a number of things over which she and Lucy had failed to agree, and regarding which Antonia had followed her own inclinations. Now, for the first time, she admitted to certain qualms.

Her anxiety was needless. When they had inspected the whole house and were once more in the drawing-room, he took her hand and kissed it with a flourish.

"I make you my compliments, m'dear. Your taste is faultless."

She flushed with pleasure. "I am glad that you approve. I have spent a great deal of money."

He lifted a mocking eyebrow. "You expect me to quarrel with you on that account?"

"No," she replied with a touch of humour, "but my grandfather may well do so."

"Sir Charles, I imagine, will not object to anything which adds to his family's consequence. He would not, for example, wish our establishment to be in any way inferior to Roger Kelshall's."

"I agree!" There was bitterness now in Antonia's voice. "On the other hand, he is likely to object most strongly to anything which makes *me* happy."

"And are you happy, Antonia?" Geraint was fingering the little ruffle of lace and ribbon she wore about her throat. "Have I begun to atone at last for the wrong I did in marrying you?"

He still spoke lightly, but there was an underlying seriousness in his voice that frightened her. She had already felt some trepidation at leaving the Mountworths' house for the privacy of their own home, and now that vague uneasiness crystallised into real alarm. She moved quickly away from him, saying breathlessly:

"Of course I am far happier than I was at Kelshall Park. I have friends, amusements, and now, for the first time in my life, a home of my own. Do not think I am ungrateful."

He laughed, too experienced to persist in the face of her obvious dismay. "I am not sure that gratitude to me is particularly apt. With the best will in the world, I could have provided neither home nor entertainment had Sir Charles not furnished the means—but I'll not presume to suggest you should feel grateful to *him*."

"You would suggest it in vain." Antonia laughed, too, with relief at this return to his normal bantering manner. "My strongest emotion towards him at present is satisfaction; not only at having escaped from him, but also at the mortification he must be feeling at having unintentionally provided me with the means to do so. Now I must go and see if Turner has finished unpacking my clothes."

It was something, Geraint reflected when she had gone, that she was learning to laugh; that the shadows were beginning to lift so that she could be young and carefree at last. Something, but not enough. He would not be satisfied until the past had been forgotten and she accepted their marriage in all its aspects. It was a challenge he could not resist, for they could scarcely have had a less auspicious beginning, and he was determined to overcome Antonia's hostility and to win her to willing surrender. That resolve, coupled with a vague feeling that he owed her at least the escape from her grandfather which she so passionately desired, had prompted him to bring her to London and to play the part of attentive bride-groom, but as time passed this had ceased to be a consciously assumed role. Now, with a wry grin for the irony of it, he could admit to himself that he was becoming more and more deeply attached to his reluctant bride.

The winning of Antonia was no easy matter. Her moods were unpredictable, and he could never be sure how she would respond to any overture. She possessed no jewels, but when, soon after their arrival in London, he gave her a pair of very fine ruby and diamond ear-rings, she eyed the gift suspiciously.

"Why should you give me jewels?"

"Why should I not?" Deliberately he kept his voice light and teasing. "Most brides are given their husband's family gems, but all the St. Arvan heirlooms went to the Jews long since. So I have bought these for you. I think you will find them becoming."

She thanked him rather ungraciously, and though these were the first trinkets of any value she had ever owned, put them away in a drawer without even trying them on.

He was disappointed, but a few evenings later, when Lucy gave a card-party, he saw that Antonia was wearing the gems.

Encouraged by this, he had since bought her other gifts, which were sometimes received with delight, more often with apparent indifference. In the same way her attitude towards him was constantly changing. At times they seemed to be approaching an understanding, but then something would happen to rouse her fierce temper or plunge her into sullen antagonism. Frequently, he knew, he was to blame for this. His tendency to see the humorous side of a situation, his habit of treating even serious matters with irreverent laughter, was something she could not readily accept; the baleful influence of Sir Charles, and the effect of her grim and haunted childhood, were still too strong.

Antonia had been looking forward to entertaining in her own house, and soon proved to be an excellent hostess. Some of the first guests to be invited to Brook Street were Mr. and Mrs. Roger Kelshall, for she had been at some pains to demonstrate that she did not share her grandfather's prejudice. She issued the invitation and then told Geraint, rather defiantly, that she had done so, but he raised no objection. They had all met once or twice at various social functions since the day Kelshall called on Lady Mountworth, and always Roger was urbane and smiling, treating his young kinswoman and her husband with exactly the right blend of warmth and reserve. Geraint did not like Mr. Kelshall, but he could appreciate the aplomb with which the elder man had accepted what must have been a galling defeat at Sir Charles's hands. It was to Antonia's advantage to be on comparatively friendly terms with her relatives, and he was prepared to tolerate a measure of cordiality.

So he made Mr. and Mrs. Kelshall welcome and, with the exception of one small lapse when his sense of the ridiculous got the better of him, carried out the duties of host in an exemplary manner. The lapse occurred when Mrs. Kelshall made a passing reference to Vincent, and Antonia, with a challenging glance at Geraint, immediately remarked:

"I have not seen my cousin these three weeks past. I trust that all is well with him?"

"Quite well, I believe," Mrs. Kelshall replied. "He has gone into the country."

"At this time of year, madam?" Geraint's surprise might have been genuine or merely assumed. "You astonish me! I did not take him for a keen sportsman."

"He has gone to visit his maternal grandmother, Lady Blackland," she explained, and glanced at Antonia. "I fear he found that to remain in London aroused emotions too painful to be borne. I am sure that I need say no more."

"Perhaps," Roger put in blandly, "St. Arvan has never had the misfortune to suffer a romantic disappointment."

"You flatter me, sir," Geraint said ironically; then he laughed. "But when I did, I confess it never occurred to me to seek sympathy from my grandmother. I perceive that Cousin Vincent is an original."

Antonia looked up, her eyes flashing; but before she could speak, Mrs. Kelshall said hurriedly:

"Vincent's mother died when he was born, and he spent much of his childhood with Lady Blackland. She is deeply attached to him, and he to her."

"An attachment which, I fear, has led her to indulge the boy more than is good for him," Kelshall added. "Her ladyship never had a son. Vincent's mother was her only child."

Geraint looked thoughtfully at him. The tone had been non-committal, but he sensed an irritation beneath the words, a resentment of Lady Blackland's influence over her grandson. Vincent could have been only two or three years old when his father was obliged to leave England, so that his formative years must have been spent in her ladyship's care. Perhaps Kelshall blamed that fact for his son's lack of spirit and his romantic notions. Roger himself was, in his own way, as forceful and autocratic as Sir Charles himself.

Sir Charles's own warning against Roger, Geraint had dismissed from his mind, laughing at himself for even half believing it. Kelshall was undoubtedly furious that the old man's fortune had passed outside the family when it could so easily have been his son's, but that was understandable and it was absurd to imagine that he would make any attempt to recover it. His second wife had been a considerable heiress and Roger now had wealth and an assured position in society; it was unthinkable that he might risk everything in a murderous attempt to add to his fortune, and only a mad old man like Sir Charles would seriously entertain such a suspicion. Amid the feudal gloom of Kelshall Park even Geraint himself had wondered for a moment if such a suspicion could be justified, but in the prosaic surroundings of fashionable London the idea became merely laughable.

A spell of warm, dry weather had improved the condition of the roads, and Geraint recollected his intention of taking Antonia to meet his one remaining relative. She went unwillingly, the thought of visiting an elderly gentleman inevitably calling up a picture of her grandfather, but she found that her fears were needless. Mr. Redfern was a kindly old man with a merry eye and a lively sense of humour, and though the modest size of his household hinted at straitened circumstances, and physical frailness at failing health, the warmth of his welcome left nothing to be desired. Living retired, he was unaware both of Geraint's imprisonment and the circumstances of his marriage, but he was so plainly delighted by the match that Antonia had not the heart to disillusion him. It could do no harm, she decided, to play for one day the part of a happy bride.

She found this surprisingly easy to do, and realised with astonishment that she was enjoying herself, so that when, at parting, Mr. Redfern urged them to visit again soon, she agreed without hesitation. Later, as their chaise headed once more towards London, Geraint said suddenly:

"In the old gentleman's state of health it would not do for him to know the true story of our marriage, and I am grateful to you for saying nothing. Thank you."

"Why in the world should I tell him? It could serve no useful purpose." She looked curiously at him. "If you feared that I might, why did you not warn me against doing so before we reached his house?"

He laughed. "I can think of no more certain way, m'dear, of ensuring that you did tell him."

She turned her head sharply away to look through the window beside her, and after a pause said in a low voice: "Do you then think me utterly selfish, utterly despicable? So ready to cause distress to those who have never done me the least harm?"

"I *think*," he replied humorously, "that when your temper is provoked you do not pause to reason at all, and I *know* that any attempt on my part to exert authority over you would most certainly provoke it."

She flushed, but spoke defiantly. "Is that so strange, considering the means by which such authority was bestowed upon you?"

"Still so unforgiving?" he said ruefully. "How long will it be, I wonder, before you forget the circumstances of our wedding?"

"Do you think it is easy to forget? Can you not conceive what it meant to me to be told, without warning, that in an hour I was to be married to a stranger, a man who had been brought from one of London's most notorious prisons to be my husband? Can you even imagine what my feelings were?" She paused, but Geraint made no reply. "And afterwards, in the library—I shall never forget how terrified I was then. I did my best to hide it, but I was sick with fear behind my bold words."

Geraint took the hand nearest to him and raised it to his lips. "My poor darling," he said with a fleeting smile, "there was no need."

She coloured, and her fingers trembled in his, but she said with some spirit: "How could I know that? Sir Charles, you may depend, had presented your character to me in a most unfavorable light. Though I have learned since that he lied, I can forgive neither him nor you for the manner of my marriage."

"Weddings take place every day," he said quietly, "in which the couples know little more of each other than we did, and perhaps have as little inclination to marry, yet they contrive to deal tolerably well together. Is it beyond all reason to hope that we may do the same?"

"Is it beyond all reason," she retorted, "to say that we already do?"

"Because we have learned to be civil to one another?" There was gentle mockery in Geraint's voice. "That is not what I meant, and you know it. Do you honestly believe that the present state of affairs can continue indefinitely?" She tried to jerk her hand away, but instead of letting her go he tightened his hold and put his other arm about her shoulders, looking down into her frightened face. "I will admit that I acted unworthily in marrying you as I did. When I learned what Sir Charles intended, I should have refused for your sake instead of agreeing for my own, but no matter how strange the manner in which the knot was tied, you are my wife, Antonia, and you cannot keep me for ever at arm's length. If you cannot forgive, then, by Heaven, you shall forget!"

"Geraint, I beg of you!" She tried to push him away. "Let me go!"

He laughed and shook his head. "That I will never do, no matter how bitterly you think you hate me." He was still holding her; his kisses stifled her protests, and for a moment or two she was quiet in his arms. His lips moved gently across her throat and he said with laughter in his voice: "And hate and love, sweetheart, are such extremes that they may sometimes be confused."

With a sudden return of panic she began to struggle wildly. "Let me go! Oh, Geraint, please!"

His grip slackened; she dragged herself free, away from his caressing hands, and pressed her own hands to her hot cheeks. Her alarm had been due as much to herself as to him; to the sudden realisation of how greatly, during the past weeks, her feelings towards him had changed. She had been unprepared for the discovery, and now felt utterly confused.

After a minute or two she ventured to look at him again. He was leaning back with folded arms in his own corner of the chaise, and as her glance met his he said curtly:

"You have nothing to fear from me, now or ever. I am not that great a villain."

She could not tell whether he were hurt or merely angry, and only knew that she wanted him to be neither. She laid her hand timidly on his arm.

"Geraint, forgive me! I cannot tell what I feel for you. Perhaps you are right, and hatred can be confused with

love. I do not know. I have known so much of one, and
so little of the other." She hesitated, and the dark eyes,
lifted to his, were no longer defiant, but pleading. "You
will be patient, will you not, and let matters between us
remain as they are—for a time?"

His expression softened, and he covered her hand with
his own. "I have given you my word that you have nothing to fear," he said in a wry tone, "and I will abide by
that, but I am not by nature a patient man, Antonia. Do
not ask me to wait too long."

One morning towards the end of April, the columns of
the *London Gazette* bore an announcement of the be-
trothal of Jessica Chalgrove to the Earl of Dereham. Antonia saw it first, and waited with some anxiety to see
what Geraint's reaction would be, but if it caused him to
feel any pang of regret he concealed it admirably. Point-
ing the announcement out to her, he said with a grin:

"So Mrs. Chalgrove prevails at last! I'll wager she is a
happy woman today."

"And Miss Chalgrove?" Antonia could not resist the
question. "Is *she* happy, do you think?"

He gave her a straight look. "If she is not," he said deliberately, "I have no doubt she will find ample consola-
tion in a countess's coronet. She is a worldly creature,
however much she may choose to pretend otherwise."

Antonia, reading into his words a bitterness they entirely lacked, suddenly lost all inclination to pursue the
matter. Perhaps, after all, it was Jessica's worldliness, and
not Geraint's chivalry, which had prevented the elope-
ment that Mrs. Chalgrove had dreaded; perhaps he had
desired it, but Jessica, though infatuated with him, had
not let her heart rule her head to the extent of sacrificing
the rank of peeress. Antonia recalled Lucy's assertion that

Geraint never wore his heart on his sleeve, and the disquieting thought occurred to her that his present careless attitude, like his continued flirtation with Jessica, might be a mask for a hurt deeper than he cared for anyone to guess.

The thought cast an unaccountable depression over her spirits, complicating yet further her already confused emotions. Starved all her life of even the simplest affection, and with only the mild attraction she had felt for Vincent to judge by, she was frightened by the force of the feelings Geraint aroused in her. These had from the moment of their first meeting been violent. Hatred, fear, anger at the wrong he had done her by accepting Sir Charles's bargain, had been succeeded by contempt for his trifling with Jessica Chalgrove and others. Now she did not know what she felt, save that he was seldom out of her waking thoughts and a constant intruder upon her dreams; that she was at all times acutely aware of his physical presence; and that the sight of him paying court to other women filled her with a fury which could barely be concealed.

In self-defence she had retreated behind a barrier of aloofness, feigning an indifference she did not feel, for she knew instinctively that to give way to these turbulent emotions would be to commit herself irrevocably, to surrender that inner citadel of the spirit which alone had enabled her to survive her harsh, unnatural upbringing. It was a surrender she could not find the courage to make.

Depression was still weighing upon her that evening, when she and Geraint went together to attend a rout-party given by Mrs. Kelshall. It made her feel tense and on edge, and though she knew she was looking her best in a new gown of rose-coloured taffeta, with the pearls which were Geraint's latest gift to her entwined in her powdered hair, the knowledge did little to improve her spirits and she made no response when he complimented her on her appearance.

The salons were already crowded when they arrived, the babble of voices almost drowning the music of the violins, but one of the first people Antonia saw was Vincent. He was standing just inside the main salon and had obviously been watching for her, for he immediately detached himself from the group about him and hurried forward. She had not known that he was back in London, and this unexpected encounter, with Geraint present, threw her into confusion. She flushed and stammered, and was furious with herself for doing either.

"I am happy to see you, cousin." Very much aware of Geraint's ironical regard, she withdrew the hand which Vincent had clasped with more warmth than formality. "I thought you were still out of town."

"I returned last night. When I waited upon my step-mother today she told me that you would be among her guests this evening." He acknowledged Geraint's presence with a curt nod. "Servant, St. Arvan."

"Yours, my dear cousin," Geraint murmured, and watched with deepening amusement Vincent's involuntary stiffening. "How very fortunate that you returned to town in time to give us the pleasure of your company."

An angry flush darkened Vincent's face, but before he could reply another acquaintance joined them. They all stood chatting for several minutes, until a minor stir was created by the arrival of Jessica Chalgrove and her mother, escorted by the Earl of Dereham. At once the newly betrothed pair were surrounded by friends and acquaintances, and Vincent looked at Geraint.

"Congratulations appear to be in order," he remarked with a hint of malice. "Do you not intend to add yours?"

With his laced handkerchief Geraint flicked a speck of dust from his sleeve of dull yellow satin. "Of course!" he said lightly, and offered his arm to Antonia. "Come, m'dear, let us not appear backward. Though," he added in a lower tone as they moved away, "if congratulations are in order, it's Mrs. Chalgrove who should receive 'em."

Jessica and her mother were seated now on a sofa between two windows, with Dereham standing beside them. Mrs. Chalgrove looked triumphant and his lordship smug, but Jessica, in a gown of her favourite blue, was pale beneath her rouge and there was a strained expression in her eyes. She was at that moment receiving the good wishes of an imposing dowager, but when she saw Geraint and Antonia approaching, her smile faded and her hand clenched suddenly on the fan she was holding.

There was a momentary and expectant hush, a suspension of talk and laughter which lasted barely the space of a heartbeat yet was as significant as a thunderclap. Jessica's gaze was fixed with painful intensity on Geraint's face, and Antonia wanted more than anything else to look at him, too, but to do so would betray the uncertainty she was determined to hide. It was for her to speak first; she did so, and was pleased to find that her voice sounded calm and untroubled.

"Permit me to wish you happy, Miss Chalgrove, and to offer you, my lord, my warmest congratulations."

"I echo those sentiments," Geraint added as Jessica murmured an almost inaudible response. "You are a fortunate man, Dereham."

His lordship acknowledged the remark sourly. He suspected St. Arvan of mockery, and any satisfaction he might have felt at winning Miss Chalgrove's hand from him was made meaningless by the fact that Geraint had already found himself a bride as beautiful and as richly endowed as Jessica herself.

Some new arrivals joined the group, and Geraint and Antonia moved away. A very young gentleman who had conceived a hopeless passion for Antonia the first time he

met her came eagerly to greet her, and, Geraint's attention being at that moment claimed by one of his cronies,
they drifted apart. Both had many acquaintances among
the crowd of guests who stood or sat or strolled about the
salons, and more than two hours passed before Antonia
had occasion to wonder what had become of her husband.

By that time her youthful admirer had drunk enough
wine to overcome his inherent bashfulness, and, contriving to draw her a little apart from the company into a
curtained alcove, poured out an impassioned declaration
of his feelings. This was the sort of situation with which
she had not yet learned to cope, but with which Geraint,
had he been at hand, would have dealt promptly and effectively. For once he was not at hand, nor could she recall having seen him in the salons for some time. In desperation she thrust past the infatuated youth, leaving him
for a moment nonplussed, and threaded her way through
the company towards the door as quickly as she could
without attracting attention.

It had occurred to her that Geraint might be in the library, transformed for the evening into a card-room, on
the ground floor, or in the adjoining room where refresh-
ments were laid out. She went downstairs, but a quick
glance into the dining-room was sufficient to show that he
was not there, and she was turning towards the card-
room when she caught a glimpse of her young admirer at
the head of the stairs. He was looking eagerly about, but
for the moment she was screened from him by two gentlemen strolling past, and she drew back quickly under the
curve of the staircase, remembering, from a previous visit
to the house, that this would enable her to reach the door
of a small anteroom.

The door, standing slightly ajar, swung silently open as
soon as she touched it. The little room beyond was illuminated only by the candles in the hall behind her, and
moonlight streaming between undrawn curtains, but this

was sufficient to show her the couple who stood very close together near the window. The rich gleam of yellow satin which was the man's coat; the glimmer of a blue silk gown; the pale blur of powdered hair. As Antonia, her own presence unsuspected, stood rigid with shock, Jessica said in a fierce whisper:

"I tell you your marriage means nothing to me, no more than my promise to Dereham. I agreed to marry him only to escape from Mama's constant prying, and to have the freedom a married woman enjoys, with no chaperone constantly at her elbow. Once I am wed, we can easily contrive to meet . . ."

Antonia turned sharply away, forgetting the tiresome youth she had been trying to evade, forgetting everything except the blazing fury, the almost intolerable hurt, which that glimpse of Geraint and Jessica had aroused. Vincent, emerging at that moment from the card-room, saw her coming towards him, her face paper-white, her dark eyes seeming to smoulder with the intensity of her anger. She looked, he thought poetically, like an avenging goddess.

"Antonia!" He went to her, laying a hand on her arm to stop her walking blindly past him. "What is it? What has happened?"

For an instant she looked at him as though he were a stranger, and he realised that she was trembling with emotion. Then her gaze focused upon him; she said in a shaking voice:

"I am going home."

"You are unwell!" Vincent's voice was full of concern. "Shall I fetch my stepmother?" She shook her head, and he added unwillingly: "St. Arvan?"

"No!" This time Antonia spoke with suppressed violence. "Just send for my carriage. I am going alone."

"I'll not permit that, when you are so distressed," Vincent said with unusual firmness. "I will escort you."

He turned to the servants and sent one to summon the

carriage, another to find Mrs. St. Arvan's wrap. When both these errands had been completed he turned to Antonia, who all the while had stood silent, absorbed in her own stormy emotions, and touched her gently on the arm.

"Come, my dear," he said gently.

Like a blind woman she placed her hand on his proffered arm and let him lead her across the hall. The lackeys flung open the door, Vincent and Antonia passed into the street, and from the head of the stairs the Earl of Dereham thoughtfully watched their departure.

Antonia sat before the mirror in her dressing-room, staring at her reflection but seeing only two figures in a shadowy room, two heads close together. Her fury had burned itself out and now only an aching wretchedness remained.

She had submitted indifferently to the attentions of her maid, oblivious for once of the woman's thin-lipped disapproval. Turner had spent all her life in service at Kelshall Park, and bitterly resented the changed circumstances which had brought her to London, forced her to keep these late hours, and to care for the frivolous, expensive clothes to which, in her opinion, the "gipsy brat" had no shadow of right. In grim silence she had undressed her mistress, put her into a light, lace-trimmed robe, draped a powdering-gown about her shoulders, and was now engaged in brushing the scented powder from her hair. She plied the brush with unnecessary violence, tugging spitefully at the glossy black tresses, but Antonia was too wrapped in misery to care.

A brisk footstep sounded in the corridor and Geraint came into the room. For a moment his glance met Antonia's in the mirror, and then he looked at the servant.

"You may go," he said curtly.

With a small, sour smile Turner laid down the brush,

curtsied, and went out. Geraint walked forward until he stood by the dressing-table, looking down at his wife. He was clearly very angry, for the blue eyes were hard and bright, the fine mouth set in a forbidding line.

"Perhaps, madam," he said abruptly, "you will have the goodness to explain why you walked out of your cousin's house in that unmannerly fashion, without even a word of farewell to your hostess. And—which is of more immediate interest to me—why you did so in the company of Vincent Kelshall."

The accusation implicit in the latter words stung her to answering indignation. "Vincent escorted me home. If he informed you of that, no doubt he informed you also that I felt unwell."

"He did not inform me. I was told of it by Dereham—damn his impudence! Kelshall did not return to his father's house after he left it with you, as no doubt you are aware." He glanced meaningly at the door of her bed-chamber, on to which the dressing-room opened. "Is he still here?"

The insult, and the injustice of it, fanned the embers of her fury to life again. She sprang to her feet, the powdering-gown slipping from her shoulders.

"No, he is not," she said furiously. "He escorted me to the front door, and then left. Do not judge his conduct, or mine, by your own!"

"What, pray, is that supposed to mean?" Geraint's voice was dangerously quiet.

"It means that instead of seeking to arouse suspicion against me, Lord Dereham would have been better employed in looking to the conduct of his promised wife. Conduct which would shame a tavern-wench! You say I was discourteous! What should be said of a woman who plights troth with one man, with the avowed intention of becoming the mistress of another?"

Now he was startled as well as angry; his eyes narrowed and he took a pace forward. "Who told you that? Kelshall?"

"Nobody told me, or needed to! I saw you with her in the anteroom, heard what she was saying. No, I was not spying on you! I was seeking somewhere to conceal myself from young Rigby, who was pestering me with drunken attentions. What I heard then told me all I needed to know."

"It told you only half the tale! Had you lingered a moment you would have heard me tell her that I want no part in such contriving. That the Countess of Dereham may favour whom she pleases, but it is an honour which I decline."

"And to tell her that, it was of course necessary to steal away with her into a darkened room?" Antonia retorted scornfully.

"It was damned necessary," he replied feelingly. "She was becoming overwrought, threatening to create a scene, and you can imagine the kind of scandal *that* would have provoked. I had an infernally uncomfortable ten minutes of it, and no sooner was that over than I found *you* had done your best to set tongues wagging by flouncing off with young Vincent."

"So now *I* am in the wrong!" Antonia's voice trembled with anger. "That is of a piece with all the rest! You may behave as scandalously as you choose, but I may not even accept my kinsman's escort home from a party."

"Not when you have attended that party in my company, or when your departure gives rise to impertinent comment. I warned you once—and I make no apology for repeating it—that since you bear my name you will conduct yourself becomingly."

"And since you are so concerned about the St. Arvan name," she flashed, "it is a pity you have not more care of your own conduct, which is far more likely than mine to bring disgrace upon it."

For a second or two he looked at her, his eyes hard as sapphires, his mouth grim; then he said softly: "Be careful, Antonia. I take that tone from no one, not even you."

"Even I?" She gave a little laugh, angrily scornful. "Oh, I look for no special privileges, sir! I am not Miss Chalgrove."

She started to turn away, but he gripped her by the shoulders and swung her round again to face him. "Once and for all," he said angrily, "let us have a clear understanding where Jessica Chalgrove is concerned. A year ago I paid court to her, as to any fashionable beauty; as a dozen other men were doing at that time. I was not in love with her, nor did I covet her fortune. My fault lay in expecting her to treat the comedy as lightly as I did, and God knows I never gave her any reason to suppose otherwise! The affair, such as it was, ended when I was thrown in prison, and I have not the smallest desire to resume it, either with Miss Chalgrove or the Countess of Dereham."

"Yet she can scarcely be blamed for supposing that you do! Your gallantry towards her leads the whole world to suppose it!" Antonia tried to move away but his grip tightened, bruising her shoulders through the thin silk. She looked up at him with blazing eyes. "Do you imagine that you have to explain your conduct to me! I care not where you bestow your favours, but I will not be taken to task for my own behaviour when I have done nothing to deserve it."

"Do you not care?" Geraint was looking intently into her face. "Do you not, Antonia?"

She turned her head quickly away, unwilling now to meet his eyes. To be sure, she cared. She could see, with piercing clarity, that her anger had its root in jealousy, and that to lay for ever the ghost of his supposed love for Jessica mattered more than anything in the world. Every instinct was urging her to believe him.

Suddenly she became intensely aware of the silence of
the house, of the intimacy of this moment when she and
Geraint were alone as they had never been before. As she
stood with averted head she could see their reflection in
the nearby pierglass, and her own disarray, with her hair,
still streaked with powder, tumbled about her face, and
the flimsy robe slipping from her shoulders, added to her
confusion. She felt defenceless, robbed of the aloof dignity behind which she had lately sought to hide, her anger
disarmed by the sudden change in his voice, and in the
way he was looking at her.

"I give you my word," he said quietly after a moment,
"that Jessica means nothing to me. If she did, I would not
single her out by empty gallantry."

"It is not Geraint's way to wear his heart on his
sleeve." An echo of Lucy's words sounded in Antonia's
thoughts, bringing hope, and, with it, the courage once
more to meet his eyes.

"I accept your word," she said breathlessly. "You have
never given me any cause to doubt it."

"I am like to do so now!" His voice was not quite
steady, and his arms went round her, gripping her against
him in a hold there was no escaping. "Once before I gave
you my word, but there are some promises, my love, too
hard for a man to keep."

His lips were on hers, ardent and demanding, over-
coming her involuntary resistance. Just for a moment she
fought against him, and then with an incoherent murmur
slid her arms about his neck and resisted no more.
Doubts, fears, even conscious thought itself, were overwhelmed, and she made no protest as he picked her up
and carried her into the bedchamber.

Part Three

Antonia, arranging spring flowers in a graceful vase, hesitated with the last blossom in her hand, considered her handiwork and then with a little nod slid the bloom into place.

"There!" she said to her attendant abigail. "Set those below the mirror yonder. The violets which Mr. St. Arvan sent me I will put in the small bowl, for the table by my sofa."

She was smiling to herself as she arranged the violets, for she was happier than she had ever been in her life; happier than she had known it was possible to be. As the spring days lengthened, her delight in life and love increased, until she felt that in all her twenty-one years this was the first real spring she had ever known; she could even think with gratitude of her grandfather, although she knew that her happiness was the last thing he desired.

Yet she could not entirely shake off the shadows of her past, even now when she was enfolded in the warmth and security of Geraint's love. At the back of her mind there lurked always a fear, a small, superstitious dread that this happiness was too complete, too perfect to last. She was ashamed of it, too much ashamed to share it even with Geraint, but try as she would she could not cast it out. It persisted, a mocking imp of a fear, the one small, secret flaw in her contentment.

As she set the bowl of violets on the table, Geraint came into the dressing-room. He carried a letter in his hand, and Antonia, quick to notice that he looked troubled, signed to the maid to leave them. The girl, a tall, buxom creature of about her mistress's age, obeyed meekly, but with a saucy upward glance at Geraint's face as she passed him. Momentarily diverted, he watched her go out and then raised an inquiring eyebrow at his wife.

"A new abigail, love? What became of the dragon you brought from Gloucestershire?"

Antonia laughed. "I sent her back. She was hopelessly unfashionable." She made a little grimace. "No, that is not the whole truth! I wanted to be rid of every reminder of my grandfather's household. This girl, Hannah Preston, came with excellent references, and suits me admirably." She sat down on the sofa and held out her hand to him. "What is wrong, my dear? You did not come merely to discuss the servants."

He took her hand and pressed a kiss on the palm as he sat down beside her. "No," he said with a sigh. "This note is from my uncle's housekeeper. The old gentleman is ill, and wants me to go to him immediately."

"Geraint!" Her fingers tightened on his in quick concern. "Is it a serious illness?"

"I trust not. I have had such a summons more than once and found when I reached him that it was a false alarm, but I dare not take the risk of disregarding it. If I did not go, and his illness proved fatal, I should never forgive myself."

"Of course you must go," she agreed at once. "Would you like me to come with you?"

"I should like it above all things," he replied with a smile, "but I'll not drag you with me on what is probably a fool's errand. I've no doubt you have engagements . . ." He broke off, snapping his fingers. "Damnation! This is the night of Lady Pettigrew's ball, is it not?"

Antonia nodded, trying to conceal her disappointment. She had been looking forward eagerly to the first masked ball she had ever attended, but if Geraint were unable to go with her most of her pleasure would be lost.

"I will make your excuses," she said in a determinedly cheerful tone. "If your uncle has need of you it must take precedence over any ball."

"If I were certain he does need me I'd not begrudge the visit, but ten to one this is just another of his starts. Devil take it! Why did it have to happen today?"

"I suppose," she suggested diffidently, "that you could not return in time for the ball, if you find he does not really need you? It is early yet, and if you ride to Barnet instead of taking the chaise you should make good time. Oh, Geraint, please!"

He slid his arm behind her shoulders, his laughing glance searching her face. "What can *my* presence matter? At these affairs you are usually so surrounded by admirers that I cannot come near you."

She gave a little ripple of laughter. "Oh, unjust! And even if I am, they all take fright as soon as you approach. They have a most lively fear of you."

"As well they may!" He still spoke teasingly, but his eyes belied the lightness of the words. "I brook no rival, sweetheart."

"You need fear none, either," she whispered, and lifted her face for his kisses. Against his lips she murmured: "And you will return tonight, my love? My dearest love!"

"I will return," he promised. "The devil himself shall not keep me away." He kissed her again, but at last, with a sigh, let her go and rose to his feet, saying ruefully: "Fiend seize my uncle! He will expect me to spend some time with him, so I had best set out with no more delay."

She clung to his hand, reluctant even now to let him go. "But you will return to me tonight, no matter how late? You promise?"

"I promise," he agreed, "unless the old gentleman is so ill I cannot leave him, but in that event I will send word."

Antonia passed the day pleasantly enough. A visit to a milliner, morning calls made and received, a promenade with Lucy in St. James's Park filled the hours until it was time to dress for the ball. The Mountworths, who were also among Lady Pettigrew's guests, took Antonia up with them in their carriage for the short journey to her ladyship's house in Hanover Square, Lucy having learned from her friend of Geraint's absence.

As usual, Antonia did not lack gallants, but though she danced, and talked gaily enough, she glanced frequently towards the door, and as time passed and Geraint did not appear, her high spirits gradually deserted her. By the time the ball drew to a close her smile had become purely mechanical, and she greeted with relief Lucy's suggestion that they should be among the first to take their leave, for now uneasiness was beginning to mingle with her disappointment.

She spoke little during the drive back to Brook Street, and her growing anxiety communicated itself to her companions sufficiently for them both to accompany her into the house. The porter informed them that Mr. St. Arvan had neither returned nor sent any message, and Mountworth, with a glance at Antonia's white face, took matters into his own hands and escorted both ladies up to the drawing-room before either could make any comment.

"I cannot understand it," Lucy remarked. "It is not like Geraint to break a promise. Do you suppose any mishap has befallen him?"

Peter directed a quelling glance at her and then addressed Antonia, who had gone to stand before the fireplace. "Do not concern yourself too much," he said reassuringly. "His message may have miscarried, or, if his uncle is indeed very ill, he may have had no opportunity to send one."

Before she could reply, the sound reached them of a loud knocking on the front door. There was a murmur of voices below, and then uncertain footsteps ascending the stairs. The door of the drawing-room opened, and Geraint himself stood swaying on the threshold.

Though his long riding-cloak still shrouded him almost to the heels, he was hatless, and a lock of hair, escaping from the ribbon to fall untidily across his brow, lent him a rakish and dishevelled appearance. For a few seconds he stood there, surveying them with a somewhat lazy eye, and then he thrust the door shut and advanced unsteadily into the room. Ignoring the Mountworths, he addressed Antonia, who had started eagerly forward to greet him.

"My dear wife," he said thickly, "I ask your pardon. I was delayed upon the road." He staggered and clutched hastily at the nearest chair to steady himself. "Unavoidably delayed," he added.

Antonia's outstretched hands dropped to her sides and she stood staring at him, the gladness in her face giving way to dismay and then to distaste, for now she could detect the reek of brandy on his breath.

"That is obvious," she said disgustedly, "and it would have been better had you remained at the tavern, where you have so obviously been amusing yourself, until you were sober again."

A sneer twisted his lips. "Admirably done, m'dear," he said sardonically, though with some slurring of the words, "but there is a question to which I must have an answer, and only you can give it." He paused, made an obvious effort to collect his wits, and then went on: "I've been neglectful, I fear! Your birthday, your coming-of-age—have I let it pass unnoticed?"

"What in the world has Antonia's birthday to do with the matter?" Lucy asked in astonishment, and Geraint laughed bitterly, though his gaze never wavered from his wife's face.

"Everything, Lucy, I fancy! Well, madam?"

"I must humour your drunken folly, I suppose," she said disdainfully. "I came of age two days ago."

"I thought so! Careless of me not to have made certain of the date. Damned careless!"

He took a step towards her, but, deprived of the support of the chair, stumbled and pitched headlong to the floor, where he lay inert, face downwards at her feet. Antonia stood staring down at him with a stricken expression, but Peter, who had been watching his friend with growing suspicion, went forward and dropped to one knee at Geraint's side. He grasped him by the shoulders and heaved him over on to his back, and the cloak, falling open, disclosed what it had until that moment so successfully concealed. Rough bandages beneath a coat torn and stained with blood.

It was past noon when Geraint opened his eyes to find Antonia, still wearing her crumpled ball-gown, dozing in a chair beside his bed. For a little while he watched her, his expression a curious blend of anguish and contempt, and then he said faintly:

"My devoted wife! How long have you kept watch over me?"

At the sound of the weak voice she started and opened her eyes. Next moment she was on her feet and bending over him.

"Geraint!" she whispered. "Oh, my love, forgive me!"

"Forgive you?" he repeated in a curious tone. "For what?"

"For my unkindness last night, when I did not know that you were hurt." She stooped, and her lips moved gently upon his. "What else is there to forgive?"

"That, madam," he replied bleakly, "lies between you and your conscience."

She drew away from him, looking at him with perplexed and frightened eyes. "I do not understand."

"Oh, have done with pretence!" he said wearily. "Your grandfather warned me, but I thought his words the delusion of a sick mind. Now I know better. Had your plan not gone awry I should now be lying dead on Finchley Common."

"*My* plan?" she stammered. "You were shot by a highwayman! That is what we were told by the postboy who drove you home."

"That is what I told my rescuers. Do you think I wish it known that my wife tried to have me murdered?"

She uttered a little cry, staring at him in white-faced horror. "Geraint, are you mad? *I* try to have you murdered?" She broke off, her expression changing, and laid a hand on his forehead; the skin felt hot and dry beneath her touch. "You have a fever! The doctor feared that this might happen, for it was madness to make the journey back to London. Oh, why did you not send word? I would have come to you."

"To complete the task left unfinished?" For all its weakness, Geraint's voice was infinitely contemptuous. "You waste no time, do you? Two days after coming of age you strike your first blow for freedom. Had your confederate been a better shot there would have been no need for a second."

Antonia put a hand to her head. She felt as though she

were in the midst of a nightmare. "Of what will you accuse me next? With whom am I supposed to have conspired?"

"Must you play the innocent, even now?" Geraint shifted his position a little, and winced. "With whom but Roger Kelshall, who covets your grandfather's fortune? To whose son you were promised when Sir Charles forced you to marry me."

"Geraint!" Her voice was pleading, and she stretched out her hand to him again. "You cannot believe that of me! I love you. Have I not given you ample proof of that?"

Neither words nor gesture won any response from him; his lips twisted in bitter mockery. "Proof of duplicity," he said, and though he spoke with difficulty she flinched from the tone he used. "That was your revenge, was it not, for the wrong I did you in agreeing to the marriage, the wrong you could not forgive? You had to be sure I loved you before delivering me into your kinsman's hands."

She stood looking down at him, her hands clasped now at her breast, her face nearly as white as his. "So little faith," she said sadly, "and yet you say you love me! What is the worth of a love which can be destroyed by a mere breath of suspicion?"

"Suspicion?" he repeated in an indescribable tone. "Who but you and I knew I would be riding across Finchley Common last night?"

She gave a gasp of dismay, remembering how she had pleaded with him to return that night, and realising how damning that appeared in the light of subsequent events. It was scarcely surprising that, afflicted by shock and pain, he had magnified that circumstance out of all proportion.

"I swear before Heaven," she said quietly, her gaze holding his without flinching, "that if my kinsman did

make an attempt on your life, he had no help from me."
She read utter disbelief in his eyes, and suddenly her
composure broke. "Oh God! Why will you not believe
me?"

She dropped to her knees beside the bed and buried
her face in her arms, shaken by passionate weeping. A
spasm of pain contracted his face; his hand moved as
though to caress her hair, then checked, and clenched
hard on the coverlet.

He was in a state of mental anguish which made his
bodily hurts seem of little account. There had been other
travellers nearby when he was fired upon from an ambush, so there was no doubt that this was a deliberate attempt at murder and not an ordinary highway robbery.
The other travellers had saved his life. They bore him to
the nearest inn, but when they would have sent for a doctor Geraint refused, and as soon as his wound had been
dressed hired a chaise to drive him back to London.
There could be no rest for him until he had confronted
Antonia.

Throughout the journey, through the pain, and the effects of the brandy he repeatedly swallowed to enable him
to stand it, grim facts had taunted him like mocking
phantoms. The would-be murderer had been waiting for
him; only Antonia knew of his intended journey; she had
urged him to make it, and to travel on horseback instead
of with the protection of carriage and servants; she had
pleaded with him to return that night. Without her help
the attempt on his life could not have been made. Those
phantoms crowded about him still, magnified by the fever
which now had him in its grip.

"Facts cannot be denied," he said in an exhausted
voice. "Kelshall may covet the fortune, but without your
help he has little hope of possessing it. Unless he were
certain of that help, he would not have tried to kill me."

With a tremendous effort Antonia checked her sobs

and sat back on her heels. For a long moment the tear-drenched dark eyes met the unyielding blue, and it was Geraint who first looked away.

"Does my word then count for nothing?" she asked wistfully. "Are you so eager to believe me treacherous and evil?" She rose to her feet and bent over him again, taking his hand in one of hers while with the other she smoothed the hair back from his brow. "These are sick fancies, my love! When you are stronger you will see them for the folly they are."

Geraint turned his head away. Physical weakness and emotional stress had brought him to the utmost limit of endurance; his certainty of Antonia's guilt was as strong as his desire to believe her innocent, and the two warring emotions seemed to be tearing him apart. He dare not look at her; her voice, her touch, the fragrance of her as she bent over him, were sheer torment.

"Leave me!" he gasped. "You cannot play the same trick twice, and desire for you will never again lead me into a trap."

The words seemed to take his last ounce of strength; his eyes closed and his face became livid in its pallor, while the sound of his laboured breathing filled the room. Frightened, Antonia turned to a small table nearby, where a draught of medicine stood ready, and, slipping an arm beneath his head, held the glass to his lips. As she did so, he opened eyes which seemed unnaturally brilliant in his white face, and with a supreme effort lifted his hand to thrust hers aside. The glass was knocked from her grasp, spilling its contents across the coverlet.

"Let be!" he whispered. "I'll take nothing . . . from hands I cannot trust."

She caught her breath and stared down at him with every trace of colour draining out of her face. Then she withdrew her supporting arm and backed away, still staring at him until, with a broken cry, she turned and fled from the room. Geraint uttered a weak, contemptuous laugh, a laugh which broke suddenly on a sob. He flung an arm across his eyes and then lay quiet, racked by an agony which had nothing to do with his wound.

Within an hour of leaving her husband's room, Antonia was at Roger Kelshall's house. She had not paused to think, to reason with herself or consider the possible consequences of her action, for she was at that moment incapable of rational thought. She only knew that the turmoil of emotion seething within her was so intense that it must find some outlet. Impossible to speak of it to the Mountworths—Geraint's friends—and so she turned instinctively to her kinsman.

Antonia's heart would ever rule her head. Her emotions were never lukewarm—she loved or hated with the full force of a passionate nature—and at that moment she felt that she hated Geraint more than any other living being. He had taught her to love him, and she had given herself utterly, in spirit, mind and body; now his accusations, his cruel disbelief, had driven her to the other extreme, to searing shame and anger, and the cruellest pain she had ever known. Intolerably wounded, she wanted nothing so much as to strike back, to hurt him as he had hurt her.

She was shown into Mr. Kelshall's study, and her cousin came across the room to greet her, taking her hand and bowing over it in his usual stately manner. "My dear Antonia, forgive me for receiving you here, but I thought it best since you say you wish to see me upon some private matter. Mrs. Kelshall is entertaining visitors in the drawing-room." Still lightly clasping her hand, he looked searchingly at her white face and smouldering eyes. "My child, what has happened to put you in such a taking?"

"Do I disguise it so badly?" She spoke jerkily, withdrawing her hand and moving away from him into the room. "Yes, something has happened. Last night my husband was shot at and wounded as he rode across Finchley Common."

"Wounded?" Kelshall's voice was sharp with concern. "My poor child, no wonder you are distressed! I trust his injury is not serious?"

"The doctor assured me that the wound is painful rather than dangerous, though it was aggravated by Geraint's insistence upon completing the journey to London. He lost much blood, and this morning is in a fever."

Roger sighed and shook his head. "What a reckless young man he is! To ride across the Common by night— and unattended, too, I have no doubt—is arrant folly. The place abounds in footpads and tobymen."

"Yes!" Antonia was still trying to speak calmly, but her actions betrayed her. She had pulled off her gloves and was jerking them fretfully between her hands. "A murder committed in such a spot would occasion little surprise."

There was a pause. Roger was looking at her with a faint frown. "I am not sure that I understand you. Are you suggesting that it was not a highway robber who attacked St. Arvan?"

"Geraint himself suggests it. He believes that a deliberate attempt was made to murder him. At your instigation."

Another pause, a longer one this time. Kelshall drew a snuff-box from his pocket and took a pinch, his expression inscrutable, his whole attention apparently fixed on the trivial action. At last he said:

"And do you believe it also? Are you here to accuse me?"

She made an impatient movement. "Of course I do not

believe it! What possible reason could you have for doing such a thing?"

"Sir Charles would say—and St. Arvan apparently agrees with him—that I covet the Kelshall fortune."

"You are in need of it, of course!" Antonia's tone was sarcastic; a gesture indicated the luxury of the room in which they stood, and his own personal magnificence. "You need money so desperately that you would risk the gallows to obtain it. Do not trifle with me, cousin, I beg!"

"I ask your pardon. Have you then come to warn me? Is it St. Arvan's intention to make some kind of charge against me?"

"No. He says he prefers the world to think that the attack was an ordinary attempt at robbery." She hesitated, staring sullenly across at him. "He believes, you see, that I conspired with you to try to kill him."

"He suspects *you?*" There was blank astonishment in Roger's voice. "In God's name, why?"

"Because only he and I knew of his intention to return from Barnet last night. Because I urged him to return— begged him, in fact—until he promised to do so, no matter how late."

She broke off abruptly and turned away, unable to trust her voice. Was it really only yesterday that promise had been asked and given? It seemed like part of another life. Through fresh waves of misery and anger she heard her cousin say:

"An unfortunate coincidence, but scarcely, one would think, conclusive evidence. Do you seek my aid in proving these allegations false? I will do everything in my power, of course, though if St. Arvan refuses to accept *your* word that you are innocent, it seems unlikely that he will be swayed by mine."

"No!" She swung again to face him, and once more anger broke through her veneer of calm, like a flame from a smouldering fire. "Do you think I will humble myself, beg and plead to be forgiven for something of which I am not guilty? If he has so little trust, if he can believe such a thing of me, after . . . Oh, let him think what he likes! I hate him! I would he lay dead at this moment!"

"My child, you do not mean that! You speak now in natural hurt and anger, but when you are calmer . . ."

"When I am calmer," she broke in viciously, "I will find a way to make him regret the wrong he has done me. You do not know—I cannot tell you—the things he has said to me today. Cruel, humiliating things which can never be forgiven." She dropped suddenly into a chair and covered her face with her hands. "And I, fool that I was, believed that he loved me!"

"My poor child!" Roger came swiftly to her side and laid his hand on her shoulder. "You are not the first woman to believe it, and I fear you will not be the last. In affairs of the heart, St. Arvan has no conscience whatsoever. It has grieved me to see you falling so completely under his influence, for I felt sure that it would bring you nothing but sorrow. You have pride, Antonia, and pride makes an ill companion for a woman bound in marriage to so shameless a libertine."

She shook her head, not looking at him. "What little pride my grandfather left me has been taken from me today. I did not know it was possible to feel such shame, such self-disgust! Oh, cousin, why did you not warn me?"

"Would you have paid any heed, my dear, if I had?" he countered gently. "There was a time, when you first came to London, when I thought you recognised your husband for what he is, but then I realised that I was mistaken. He deceived you as he has deceived so many others, and, indeed, how could it be otherwise, reared as you had been in such strict seclusion? St. Arvan has seldom encountered any difficulty in seducing other men's wives; it was only to be expected that he would enjoy a similar success with his own."

His hand still rested on her shoulder, and as he spoke he felt the gradual stiffening of her body. At last she looked up at him, and though her eyes were wet, tears could not quench the anger which blazed in them.

"There is no need to remind me, sir, of my own gullibility. I am credulous no longer, and I swear that somehow I will make him pay in full for the way he has humiliated me! I will see him humbled, made a fool of, a laughing-stock . . . !" She broke off, controlling herself with an effort, and rose to her feet. "I must go back. I should not have come, I suppose, for should he learn of it, it will but strengthen his certainty of our guilt. Forgive me, cousin, for inflicting my troubles upon you, and accept my thanks for bearing with me so patiently."

"My dear child, do not speak of thanks," he said quickly. "To whom should you turn in trouble, if not to me? My one regret is that I can do nothing to help you."

"You have helped me, sir, by allowing me to talk to you," she replied with a brave attempt at a smile. "Had I not done so, I think I would have run mad. And do not, I beg, feel any apprehension that Geraint will level accusations at you. Vanity alone will prevent him from disclosing this imagined plot between us."

"I believe you are right, my dear, and for your sake I am glad of it, for that would be but another burden for you to bear." He took her hand in both his own, and stood looking at her in a troubled way. "Would that there were some way of rescuing you from this intolerable situation, for I can see no hope of happiness for you as St. Arvan's wife. Upon my soul, Sir Charles has much to answer for!"

"That, sir, is not likely to make him sleep less soundly o' nights," she said bitterly. "My happiness has never played any part in his considerations."

"Had it done so, my child, he would never have prevented your marriage to Vincent. The boy adores you, and would have spent the rest of his life endeavouring to make you happy. Nor would he try to play the tyrant with you, as I fear St. Arvan may do if you try to defy him."

The words lingered in Antonia's mind while she bade her kinsman goodbye and was driven back to Brook Street. It was true, of course. Even from the first she had realised that if she married Vincent she would always have the governing of their affairs. It was his nature to depend always upon the stronger characters of those about him, to follow, rather than to lead; to entreat, rather than to demand. He would have been a pliant, adoring husband, attentive to her lightest wish; not one who filled her life with gaiety and laughter, taught her to love him and swore that he loved her, yet now believed her guilty of a monstrous betrayal.

She leaned her head against the velvet squabs of the carriage and closed her eyes. The blazing fury which had driven her to her cousin's house had subsided, and she felt sick at heart and desperately tired; not even the memory of Geraint's bitterly hurtful words could goad her dead fury to life again. From beneath her closed eyelids now, painful tears forced their way, to trickle down her cheeks and drop at length in small, dark splashes on the rich silk of her gown. Outside, over the grey London streets, rain began to fall.

When Mr. Kelshall returned to his study after escorting Antonia to her carriage, a man was standing beside the big desk which occupied one corner of the room. A slight, pallid man, so completely nondescript in feature and colouring that it would be difficult, when he was not present, to recall what he looked like; a quiet, self-effacing person, forming, in his discreet dark clothes, a striking contrast to Kelshall's resplendent figure.

Roger glanced at him with raised brows. "You heard, Tim?"

"Every word, sir. That was something we did not foresee."

"That St. Arvan would suspect her? No, but it is a development which may well prove to my advantage. I must do everything in my power to foster this rift between them." He smiled faintly, with the utmost contempt. "I have no doubt that my young kinswoman will prove an able, if unwitting ally in that. She is a creature of emotion."

The other man was frowning. "An emotional nature, sir, cannot always be depended upon. Suppose, when her temper cools, she feels more kindly towards her husband?"

Roger shrugged. "Unlikely, to say the least of it. There are few things more galling than to be condemned for something of which one is entirely innocent, and you may be sure that I shall neglect no opportunity of keeping her resentment alive." He sat down at the desk and leaned back in the chair, swinging his quizzing-glass to and fro on its ribbon. "Do you know, Tim, upon reflection I believe that last night's episode, far from being the failure we thought it, may prove to have laid the foundation for a far more successful scheme?"

"I hope so, sir." Timothy did not sound entirely convinced. "To my mind, it would be better if Mr. St. Arvan never recovered from his wound. If Hannah were furnished with the means, while he lies sick a-bed . . . !"

"Poison?" Kelshall shook his head. "No, no, Tim! By far too dangerous. Discovery would be almost certain. Besides, for the present the immediate urgency is past, and it will be better to tread warily. We must not forget Sir Charles."

Timothy did not pretend to misunderstand him, for he was fully conversant with the situation in the Kelshall family. His parents had been in the service of Roger's parents; he and Roger were the same age, and had been closely acquainted since early childhood; Timothy had been Roger's personal servant for nearly forty years, and now occupied a unique position in the Kelshall household. He was at once servant and friend, counsellor and confidant, and there was nothing he would not do, no crime he would not commit, to advance the interests of his master. His quiet manner masked a ruthlessness as great as Kelshall's own, and his single-minded devotion to Roger was the only admirable trait in his devious and unscrupulous character.

"What news of the old gentleman, sir?" he asked now.

"When I last inquired the state of his health, Mrs. St. Arvan informed me that, according to his chaplain, he has failed rapidly of late. He cannot live very long, but while he does, there is always the danger that he might disinherit her if she were suddenly widowed. That is a risk which, yesterday, I felt compelled to take. Today, thanks to St. Arvan's suspicions of his wife, the situation is entirely different."

"What do you mean to do, Mr. Roger? I suppose naught *can* be done until Mr. St. Arvan is about again?"

"Nothing whatsoever, Tim, save, as I have said, to nourish his wife's resentment towards him, but the situation is promising. Very promising indeed! All that remains is to consider how best to turn it to my own advantage."

Geraint and Antonia confronted one another in the drawing-room of the house in Brook Street. This was the first time he had emerged from his room since being carried unconscious to it; the first time they had met since she fled from his accusations. Since that day she had not been near him, simply keeping herself informed of his progress towards recovery. Hate him she might, but when they met again it must be upon equal terms, not while he was ill and in pain. Now the time had come, and they, who had been lovers, faced each other as enemies.

He stood tall and straight before her, a little paler, a little thinner, voice and eyes as cold as ice. "It is time we reached an understanding," he said abruptly. "You told me once that you could never forgive the manner of our marriage, and though I did not then believe you, your arguments"—one eyebrow lifted with a ghost of the old, gay mockery—"have since been forceful enough to convince me. You are my wife, and unfortunately there is no remedy—save yours—for that, but in future we will lead separate lives. You are now securely established in society and I cannot flatter myself that you have any further need of me in that respect. Have no fear that I shall trespass upon your privacy in any other."

There was a pause, while Antonia sought for words which would equal his in frigid dignity. The palms of her hands felt damp and sticky and she was shaken by a blend of relief and anger and—she had to admit it—of fear. This was Geraint as she had never before seen him, quiet and cold and infinitely dangerous. She thought suddenly that this was how he must look to an opponent facing him across the slim, crossed blades of small-swords, and as suddenly understood the circumspection with which even her most ardent admirers behaved in his presence.

"For that, at least, I am grateful," she said coldly. "I scarcely dared to hope for such forbearance, even though you have sworn that never again will you be swayed by desire for me."

In spite of her determination to betray no feeling,

something of the pain and anger that memory evoked sounded in her voice. A flicker of answering emotion showed for an instant in Geraint's eyes and he took a step towards her.

"Antonia, a sick man has strange fancies, and it seemed to me then that the trap *must* have been of your devising, yours and Kelshall's. If you had no hand in it, if I have wronged you . . ." He caught her by the shoulders and looked searchingly into her face. "In God's name, girl, tell me the truth!"

For a second or two the issue hung in the balance. At that moment a reconciliation was possible, and the gulf between them might have been bridged before it widened too far. Antonia was tempted, and the very force of the temptation hardened her heart, for the yielding, it seemed, was to be all upon her side. The accusations, the bitterly hurtful and humiliating words, the refusal to believe her protestations of innocence—these were to be forgotten, set aside, dismissed as the mere effects of injury and fever. All the resentment which, while Geraint lay ill, her kinsman had in subtle ways encouraged, rushed over her again.

"*If* you have wronged me?" she said furiously. "When have you ever done aught else? *If* you have wronged me!" She wrenched herself from his suddenly slackened hold; her voice trembled with anger and disdain. "Spare me this, I beg! You have said that henceforth we shall go our separate ways, and that suits me very well. There need be no more pretence between us!"

"So be it!" Geraint drew back, once more the cold, quiet, dangerous enemy. "Do not imagine, however, that I am giving you leave to amuse yourself as you please, for let one word of scandal attach to your name and you return to your grandfather's house—for good! Make no mistake about that."

Her anger grew as phrase followed humiliating phrase.

"I see!" she said in a voice thick with rage. "I am to sit quietly at home while you amuse yourself with Miss Chalgrove and her like. There is to be one rule of conduct for you, and quite another for me."

"Exactly!" he agreed unpleasantly. "I shall do as I please and you will do as you are bidden." She tried to argue, but he went on without giving her a chance to speak. "You have made your choice, Antonia, and we will abide by it, but upon my terms. I will not compel you to your duty as my wife, but in all other matters you will obey me."

"Obey you?" she repeated furiously. "I will see you in hell first!"

His brows lifted. "With the help of your subtle kinsman, no doubt? I thank you for the warning, and now here is one to match it. I intend to defend myself against Kelshall by every means I can devise, and if the chance offers, I shall destroy him. Whatever plot you hatch with him, remember that! I do not judge him to be a man willing to shoulder an accomplice's guilt along with his own."

To the world in general it soon became obvious that the St. Arvan household was no longer a happy or united one, and speculation concerning the match, which had died down for a time, revived with fresh vigour.

After his recovery, Geraint plunged once more into the pleasures of the town. He drank more than was good for him, lost—and won—heavily at cards and wagers, and showed an alarming tendency to pick a quarrel on the slightest provocation. Nor were these the only causes he gave for gossip. He continued to flirt outrageously with every pretty woman of his own class, while before long his name became linked, less innocently, with that of a lively young widow who lived on the fringes of society.

This lady, however, could not flatter herself that she was the only object of his attentions; there was also a dancer from the Opera House, and a young woman whose brother kept a fashionable gaming-hell, with whom she was occasionally obliged to share his favours.

The older and more staid members of polite society, some of whom had hoped that marriage would have a steadying effect upon him, regarded with disapproval his reckless philandering. Lucy, dismayed and distressed, tried to take him to task, only to have her well-meant intervention dismissed with a curtness she had never expected to meet with from Geraint, while Antonia, when approached, was more civil but equally adamant in refusing to discuss any aspect of her marriage. Lucy carried her subsequent doubts and fears to her husband, and was astonished to be told sternly not to interfere—for Mountworth was the only person to whom Geraint had confided what he believed to be the truth of his narrow escape from death.

Antonia, too, had flung herself into a feverish round of social activity, and was scarcely ever at home unless she were entertaining friends, which, combined with her husband's erratic habits, meant that sometimes days passed without them meeting beneath their own roof, though they were constantly encountering each other in public places. On the rare occasions when formality demanded that they attend some function together, they treated each other with cold civility and as soon as possible drifted apart into the company of their own particular set.

Antonia was constantly surrounded by admirers, but though her numerous gallants were eager enough to bestow upon her flowers and compliments, or to squire her to parties, their behavior was always strictly within the bounds of propriety. She had no desire to indulge in amorous intrigue, but it was galling to know that even the opportunity to do so was lacking. She had the curious fancy that the shadow of Geraint's reputation as a swordsman stood ever at her side, an invisible guardian which none of her cavaliers had the courage to defy. None, that is, until she made the acquaintance of Captain Raymond Bibury.

Their first encounter was brief and informal. She was leaving the Theatre Royal one night amid a considerable press of people, when a voice at her side said courteously:

"Your pardon, madam. I believe you have dropped your fan."

Antonia glanced round, to find a gentleman holding out to her the fan of delicately painted chicken skin which she had supposed to be still dangling from her wrist. The broken loop of ribbon hanging from it indicated plainly how it had come to fall.

"Yes, that is mine," she said with a smile. "I am very grateful to you, sir, for I should not care to lose it. Thank you."

He bowed slightly as he returned it to her. "It is a privilege, madam, to be of service to Mrs. St. Arvan."

Faintly surprised, she looked curiously at him. He was a stranger to her, a sparely built man of about thirty, a little above middle height, dressed fashionably but without extravagance. His complexion was swarthy, in striking contrast to his powdered hair, and his lean countenance, somewhat deeply lined for his age, held a look of faintly cynical humour.

"I do not think I know you, sir," she said uncertainly.

"I am not so fortunate, madam, as to be numbered among your acquaintances," he replied gallantly, "but who in London could fail to recognise the lady whose beauty is so lavishly and so justly praised? I repeat, it is a privilege to serve you."

He bowed again and moved away, disappearing into the crowd. Antonia was intrigued. The gentleman had an

air, and she found herself wondering who he was and
whether she would see him again; he was, she felt certain,
a newcomer on the fashionable scene.

Two days later, walking in the Park, she did see him
again, this time in the company of a lady with whom she
was slightly acquainted. In the ordinary way, Antonia and
Lady Hurstwood would have done no more than exchange bows, but on this occasion her ladyship paused to
greet her.

"My dear Mrs. St. Arvan, I trust I see you well? You
were not, I think, at Mrs. Fortescue's rout-party last
night?"

Antonia made some civil reply. She was a little surprised, for Lady Hurstwood was considerably older than
she, and all Antonia knew of her was that she was married to a rich and elderly valetudinarian who spent his
time at one watering-place after another; that she lived in
Curzon Street; and was famous for her card-parties, at
which the play was notoriously deep. She was very fashionable, very extravagant, and generally held to have little
interest in her own sex.

Her present affability was soon explained. When greet-
ings had been exchanged she said, with a slightly arch
smile: "My dear, you must allow me to present one who
is all eagerness to meet you, and has prevailed upon me
to perform the introduction. Captain Bibury—Mrs. St.
Arvan."

Antonia curtsied; the swarthy gentleman bowed over
the hand she extended to him, and saluted it with practised grace. Antonia introduced her own companions and
the whole group strolled on together, the Captain skilfully
ousting from Antonia's side the patched and painted beau
who had hitherto occupied that position. The beau bri-
dled indignantly, and made a spiteful comment, then,
meeting the Captain's amused yet slightly challenging

glance, subsided into sulky silence. Captain Bibury ignored him, and devoted his whole attention to Antonia.

By the time they parted he had sought and received permission to call upon her, and Antonia had decided that she liked him very well. There was a quality about him, a sort of debonair arrogance, which appealed to her, though had it been suggested that she found this attractive because in some obscure way it reminded her of Geraint, she would indignantly have repudiated so far-fetched a notion.

In the days which followed, polite society grew accustomed to seeing Captain Bibury and Mrs. St. Arvan together. He was soon her most constant cavalier, for he made no secret of his admiration for her, while she was pleased to find at last a man who did not entertain her with one eye, so to speak, on her husband's reactions.

He was not, she thought, a man who was easily intimidated. He spoke little about himself, beyond disclosing that he had lived much abroad and had only recently returned to England to take possession of an inheritance, but she gained the impression that he had seen a great deal of the world, and had been obliged, for much of his youth, to make his own way in it.

One evening, a fortnight or so after Antonia's first meeting with Bibury, she happened to encounter Roger Kelshall at a ball. Drawing her a little aside from the rest of the company, he said softly:

"Tell me, my child, are you still anxious to punish St. Arvan for his treatment of you, to humble his pride a trifle? If you are, I believe you now have at hand the means to accomplish it."

Antonia, who had just endured the humiliation of seeing Geraint dance, for the third time that evening, with Jessica Chalgrove, and was aware that the disapproving glances levelled at him on that account were surpassed only by the pitying or malicious ones directed at her, was in a mood when this suggestion appealed strongly to her. It did not occur to her that her cousin was shrewd enough to be aware of that fact.

"If I indeed have the means, sir, I beg that you will tell me what they are," she replied fiercely. "His conduct is insufferable—beyond all bearing! I will not endure it!"

"Nor need you, my dear. He behaves as he does because he believes that none dare gainsay him. Take Dereham, for example! For St. Arvan to single out Miss Chalgrove as he has done tonight, almost on the eve of her wedding, is cause enough for a quarrel between them, yet Dereham, although in the general way no coward, has prudently withdrawn to the card-room so that he may pretend ignorance of the matter. Small wonder your husband considers himself invincible."

"Perhaps he is," she said doubtfully. "He has fought many duels, has he not?"

Kelshall shrugged. "I do not deny him some skill, but let a man come victoriously through a few meetings and he acquires a reputation which makes it less and less necessary to prove his prowess. St. Arvan trades upon such a reputation." He paused to look thoughtfully at her, and then added softly: "Would it not give you infinite satisfaction, Antonia, to see the bubble of his vanity pricked, his so-called deadly swordsmanship made a mockery of, and himself an object of ridicule?"

Antonia was not looking at him. Her gaze had drifted across the room to the alcove where Geraint was now sitting with Jessica, his head bent towards hers as he murmured some remark. Jessica blushed and rapped him lightly across the knuckles with her folded fan, but her tinkling laughter came clearly to Antonia's ears.

"Infinite satisfaction, cousin," she agreed venomously, "but how could such a thing be achieved?"

Roger lifted his quizzing-glass and through it surveyed the company until his glance rested on Raymond Bibury, engaged in talk with two other men a short distance away.

"Yonder," he said calmly, "is a man who could achieve it for you."

"Captain Bibury?" Antonia was startled. "What makes you think so?"

The quizzing-glass remained poised, but Roger's glance transferred itself briefly to her face. "I was curious about Bibury and took the trouble to make some inquiries concerning him. It seems that the gallant Captain has had a somewhat chequered career. For the two years preceding his return to England, for example, he was a fencing-master in Paris."

"A fencing-master?" Antonia caught her breath. "Then if he and Geraint were to meet . . . ?"

"St. Arvan would undoubtedly suffer a most humiliating defeat. His skill may be considerable, but it cannot possibly equal that of a man who for years has made his living by his mastery of the sword. How everyone would laugh at him!"

Her eyes gleamed at the prospect, but then her face clouded again and she shook her head. "It is too dangerous! One of them might be killed."

"My dear child!" Roger laughed gently, mocking her doubts. "Bibury would not wish to make it a killing matter, for that would oblige him to leave England and his newly acquired inheritance, while St. Arvan would be fully occupied in defending himself. All he would suffer is a chastisement long overdue."

The Captain had parted from his two companions and was coming towards them. Mr. Kelshall's quizzing-glass tapped lightly, admonishingly, upon Antonia's shoulder.

"Long overdue!" he repeated quietly. "The matter rests in your hands, Antonia. Only you can bring about the necessary situation."

The suggestion made by her kinsman rapidly took possession of Antonia's mind, nourished by Geraint's own conduct. She began to encourage Bibury as she had encouraged no other man, so that soon he was seen everywhere in her company. In her box at the theatre; standing up with her to dance; walking beside her sedan-chair as it was borne through the streets. At the house in Brook Street he was a constant visitor. It was the custom for ladies of fashion to admit their more favoured admirers to their boudoirs during the latter stages of the toilette, so that the gallants might offer advice on such delicate matters as the choice of a perfume and the placing of patches, and whoever was or was not received in Antonia's dressing-room on such occasions, Captain Bibury was certain to be found there.

Inevitably there was gossip, and inevitably it came to Geraint's ears, but the effect was not at all what Antonia had hoped. He appeared unexpectedly in the dressing-room one evening, to the ill-concealed consternation of two of the three gentlemen present, both of whom obviously regarded the intrusion of a husband at such a time as ominous as it was inopportune. The third man, Captain Bibury, who was leaning elegantly against the dressing-table at which Antonia sat, while Hannah, holding an open patch-box, stood close by, merely accorded Geraint a single indifferent glance and did not pause in his dissertation on the exact position of the patch Mrs. St. Arvan was to wear.

"No, dear lady, not *la majesteuse* on the forehead—not tonight. Nor yet the *galante*. It must be—let me see! Ah, yes! Unquestionably, *la friponne!*" Shaking back his ruffles, he selected a tiny star of black silk from the box and with cool audacity pressed it into place close to Antonia's lips. "So! That is perfect!" He glanced up. "Ah, St. Arvan! Your most obedient servant, sir."

With hard eyes and smiling mouth Geraint acknowledged the greeting, complimented his wife on her gown, and begged the favour of a word with her in private before she set out for whatever entertainment she planned for that evening. She agreed, with an indifference she did not entirely feel, and when the gentlemen had withdrawn to wait for her below, and Hannah had been dismissed from the room, she said impatiently:

"Well, what is it? Pray be brief, for I am engaged to go with Lucy to Ranelagh."

The smile had vanished; the coldness in his eyes remained. "Briefly, then, the matter is this. Bibury is too much in your company. In future you will accord him no more of it than common courtesy dictates."

The peremptory command infuriated her. She said coldly: "Of what, pray, are you accusing me?"

"Of nothing more, as yet, than folly, but folly can do harm enough. When wagers begin to be laid in the clubs on the eventual success of Bibury's pursuit of you, a greater decorum on your part is imperative. He will not come to this house again."

"And if he does?"

"If he does, and you receive him, you will return straightway to Gloucestershire. And you will remain there. Kelshall Park or Brook Street—the choice, madam, is yours. It is a matter of complete indifference to me."

The threat wrung from her a sullen promise of obedience, for the thought of a return to her grandfather's house filled her with overwhelming dismay. She could not go back there. She could not! In disgrace, too, for Sir Charles would be quick to detect the reason for her return

even if Geraint did not tell him. He might even take it
upon himself to punish her, but her own plan to punish
Geraint was apparently a failure.

Her companions that evening found her in less than her
usual spirits. She paid little heed to the concert of music
they had come to hear; merely toyed with the refresh-
ments laid out in the booth; and afterwards, when the
whole party left the Rotunda to stroll through the gardens, enjoying the warm summer night, she accepted
Captain Bibury's escort abstractedly but walked in preoccupied silence, scarcely noticing whither they went.

The Captain maintained a stream of casual and amusing small-talk to which she replied very much at random,
her thoughts being fully occupied by Geraint's ultimatum
and the dilemma from which, try as she might, she could
see no means of escaping. If she defied him, he would
send her back to Gloucestershire; if she obeyed his orders
she would not only be deprived of the opportunity of humiliating him, but would herself be humiliated, for everyone would guess that her flirtation with Bibury had ended
at her husband's command.

"I fear, madam, that you are not in spirits this evening," Bibury remarked at last. "Something is troubling
you, is it not?"

He spoke in a suddenly serious tone which penetrated
Antonia's preoccupation and made her turn her head to
look at him. "Yes, it is," she said frankly, "but I ask your
pardon for allowing it to become so apparent. I am poor
company, I fear."

"That, madam, you could never be," he replied with a
smile, "but I reproach myself for failing to find the means
to raise your spirits."

She sighed. "Then reproach yourself no longer, sir. The
fault is not yours."

"No?" He glanced quizzically at her. "Then, if I may
be so impertinent as to hazard a guess, I would say that it

is, perhaps, your husband's?" She stiffened, and started to withdraw her hand from his arm, but he laid his own over it, holding it prisoner. "Forgive me! I had no right to say that, but you were not thus downcast when you first received me this evening."

Antonia glanced quickly about her; Lucy and the others were almost out of sight, and only strangers surrounded them. She halted and turned to face him. "He has forbidden me to receive you again, or to accord you more than common civility. Perhaps I should not tell you this, but I want you to know that it is not by my choice that our friendship must end."

A party of young men and women passed by, jostling about them. Bibury drew Antonia to the side of the walk, into the shadow of the trees which bordered it. "Must it end? Does he demand, and you accord him, such complete obedience?"

"He has the means to ensure it," she replied bitterly. "I obey, or I go back to my grandfather in Gloucestershire, with no hope of being permitted to return. That I could not endure! I was not happy in that house."

"To cause you unhappiness," he said slowly, "is the last thing I desire, but you are certain that this is not just an empty threat?"

"Quite certain," she said flatly, adding with a wry smile: "So you see, Captain Bibury, in either event any further friendship between us is out of the question, and you will understand, I hope, when I say that I prefer to end it thus and remain in London, rather than to be sent back to Kelshall Park like a disobedient schoolgirl."

He was silent for a moment. Beneath the trees it was too dark for her to read his expression, for his face was no more than a shadowy blue between the paleness of powdered hair above and lace below, but she had the impression that he was looking at her very hard.

"Madam, I understand," he said quietly at last. "We

both knew from the first that this would come, but believe me sincere when I say that I wish it had not come so soon." He took her hand again and raised it to his lips. "This is farewell, then. After tonight we are unlikely to meet again."

He laid her hand once more on his arm and they strolled on in the direction taken by their companions, both silent now, busy with their own thoughts. Antonia was grateful for his understanding, yet faintly piqued by the readiness with which he had accepted his dismissal, and more than a little puzzled by the finality of his last words. Their close companionship might be at an end, but in the close-knit circle of the fashionable world, surely it was inevitable that they should meet again?

Those gentlemen who witnessed the quarrel between Raymond Bibury and Geraint St. Arvan all agreed that the Captain deliberately provoked it. They were equally united in the opinion that its real source lay not in the very trivial disagreement from which it sprang, but in the recent gossip linking the names of Captain Bibury and Mrs. St. Arvan; anything else was simply a polite subterfuge to protect the lady's reputation. No one was greatly surprised, but most felt that Bibury showed an almost suicidal recklessness in risking an encounter with a man generally looked upon as one of the most dangerous swordsmen in London.

The quarrel took place on the day after the visit to Ranelagh, and the meeting was arranged for two days later, at seven in the morning in Marylebone Fields. The news spread rapidly through the clubs and gaming-houses where men of fashion foregathered, but naturally, since such matters were considered unfit for ladies' ears, the feminine half of the polite world remained in ignorance.

Roger Kelshall, however, had his own reasons for wishing Antonia to know about the duel, and sent a cryptic note round to Brook Street by the hand of one of his lackeys.

This communication was delivered to Antonia by her abigail while she was dressing for Lady Brentford's card-party. It was brief and to the point.

My dear Cousin,

It would appear that you are about to have the satisfaction you so earnestly desire, for I understand that the chastisement so long overdue is to be administered tomorrow morning at seven of the clock. Pray accept my compliments.

I am,

Yours, etc.

R.K.

Antonia sat staring at the note, unaware that Hannah was watching her with sharp, observant eyes. Roger's meaning was clear enough, but she was at a loss to understand how the situation had come about. She had supposed from Geraint's attitude that he had no thought of calling Bibury out, for that, surely, could only increase the scandal he said was brewing, and which he seemed so determined to avoid. She was puzzled, but gratified. He had treated her abominably and it would serve him right to be made to look ridiculous. Nothing could ever avenge the injustice of his accusations, or heal the wound he had dealt her, but at least he would realise that he could not play the tyrant, or dictate to her her choice of friends.

Her mood of satisfaction lasted throughout the evening, and her fellow guests at Lady Brentford's house observed that Mrs. St. Arvan, who for the past two days had appeared to be suffering from a lowness of spirits, had now made a complete recovery. Not even a run of shockingly bad luck at the cardtable succeeded in depressing her; she shrugged it laughingly aside and declared that she would soon come about.

When she returned home, however, and retired to bed, she found that, inexplicably, she could not sleep. Roger had assured her that there would be no danger in a meeting between Geraint and Captain Bibury, that the only victim would be Geraint's vanity, but suppose he were mistaken? Presumably even the most expert swordsman could sometimes make mistakes. She tossed and turned, trying in vain to recapture the mood of elation she had felt earlier and wishing, now that the matter was out of her hands, that she had never been tempted to embark upon it. At last she fell into a doze, but was troubled by confused and terrifying dreams and awoke to find herself weeping.

By half past seven she could endure inaction no longer, and got up to pace restlessly about bedchamber and dressing-room. Afraid to ring for Hannah, since to do so this early would arouse the liveliest curiosity, she could not even occupy herself with the lengthy and complicated business of dressing. An attempt to read a book was a dismal failure, since her attention refused to remain on the printed page; she tossed the volume aside and resumed her uneasy prowling. How long did it take to fight a duel? How soon could she hope to receive any news? What would the news be when it came?

It was nearly half past eight when the sound of Geraint's voice sent her flying across the dressing-room to the door. Her rooms were at the back of the house, so she had not heard him arrive home, and by the time she flung open the door he was already crossing the landing towards it. He paused, and for a second or two they stared at one another in silence, then he advanced again to grip her by the arm and thrust her before him into the room. Once inside he released her and, closing the door, leaned his shoulders against it.

His face was pale and tired and appallingly grim, and against the pallor the blue eyes blazed with anger. "Up already, my love?" he said savagely. "Would it not have been more prudent to feign ignorance of what was happening? It does not look well to appear so eager for news of your widowhood."

"My widowhood?" Antonia, rubbing her arm where he had grasped it, stared blankly for an instant before her own temper flared. "You have no right to say such a thing! There was no question . . ."

"No right?" he broke in furiously. "Do you take me for a fool? You blatantly encouraged Bibury's attentions in the hope that I would call him out, and when you found that instead I meant to send you back to your grandfather, you had him force a quarrel upon me. Only once again your plan has misfired. I can appreciate your disappointment."

"Yes, I encouraged him!" Antonia was by this time as angry as he. "I wanted you to be taught a lesson. I wanted to prove that you are not invincible, with the right to ride roughshod over anyone who opposes you. I wanted to see you humiliated and laughed at and . . ."

"You wanted me dead!" he interrupted, and so silenced her protests. "The first attempt failed, so with Kelshall's aid you hired Bibury to make a second. Would it interest you to know that this time you came within a hair's breadth of success? He is a damnably fine swordsman, the best I have ever encountered, and had chance not favoured me we should not now be having this conversation."

"You overcame him?" Antonia's voice had sunk until it was little louder than a whisper. "Geraint, he is not dead?"

"He will recover. I shall not be obliged to fly the country yet. Perhaps I should make you my apologies on that account!"

"Give thanks for it, rather," she said in a shaken voice. "Your life was never in danger. Only your pride."

He looked at her with such contempt in his eyes that she shrank from him as though he had struck her. "Spare me this hypocrisy, I beg," he said in a tone as scathing as his look. "We both know that you hate me and wish me dead. As for this morning's affair, do you think a man does not know when his opponent means to kill him? Even if I had not known, if I had never before fought in earnest, the mere fact that Bibury came to the ground in a post-chaise-and-four, with luggage strapped on the back, would be proof enough of his intentions. He was taking no chances. Had he killed me, he would have been well on his way to the coast before anyone could have prevented him."

Antonia stumbled to the sofa and sank down on it, covering her face with her hands, for an appalling suspicion was taking shape in her mind. She remembered how Roger Kelshall had suggested that she revenge herself upon Geraint by stirring up trouble between him and Bibury; how he had assured her that there could be no question of a fatal ending to such a quarrel. He had known that it was not so. He had tricked her, made use of her, brought her close to committing the very crime of which Geraint had already unjustly accused her. And if that were true of this attempt, came the sudden, horrifying thought, why not of the previous one also?

"God forgive me! What have I done?" she asked herself, and lifted an ashen face towards her husband. "Geraint, I swear before Heaven . . . !"

"Then do not," he broke in harshly, "for you would perjure yourself to no purpose. I would not believe you now if you avowed your innocence Bible in hand. If I followed my inclination I would pack you off immediately to Kelshall Park, but to send you away now would appear to confirm these damned rumours of an intrigue with Bibury. You will have to remain in London until the gossip concerning you has died down."

" 'Until' . . . ?" There was dismay in Antonia's voice. "You do not mean to send me back to that place? Oh, do not! I beg that you will not!"

He looked at her, his expression sombre. "Would to God I had never removed you from it! I should have heeded your grandfather's advice in that, as in other things, for I have come to the conclusion that he is a deal wiser than I have ever given him credit for. I shall not make the same mistake again! You will go back to him as soon as I decide that the time has come. At least that will put an end to *your* share in these plots against my life."

Part Four

As early as she could do so without occasioning remark, Antonia sent for her carriage and had herself driven to her cousin's house. As before, he received her in his study, where, seated behind the desk, he listened unmoved to her bitter accusations. Leaning back in his chair, his elbows resting on its arms and the long, gold-mounted quizzing-glass balanced between his finger-tips, he watched her from beneath drooping lids as she paced angrily to and fro before him. He seemed indifferent and even faintly amused.

"I wish you would be seated, my dear child," he drawled at length. "You look magnificent, but I am far too old to be impressed and find this restlessness intolerably fatiguing."

"Is that all you have to say?" She halted in front of him, resting her hands lightly on the edge of the desk. "You do not deny that you tricked me? That you believed Captain Bibury would kill Geraint?"

"There would be no point in denying it," he replied in a bored tone. "I had every hope—indeed, every expectation—that he would kill him, and he came within an ace of doing so. Your husband, my dear, must bear a charmed life."

"He has need to, since you are plotting against it," she said bitterly. "I suppose you will not deny, either, that the attack on Finchley Common was of your contriving?"

He inclined his head. "I will not. On that occasion, however, I did not deliberately set out to implicate you."

"Am I to thank you for that? My God, what a fool I was to come running to you for sympathy when Geraint accused me! I played straight into your hands, did I not?"

"I do not think you need reproach yourself for that," he said consolingly. "I should have learned of the situation in any event. Has it not occurred to you to wonder how I knew of St. Arvan's intention to return from Barnet that night?"

"Obviously someone told you, and there is only one person who could conceivably have discovered it, if she chanced to have her ear to the door while Geraint and I were talking. You have been bribing my abigail to spy on us."

"Something like that," he agreed with a faint smile. "It was necessary to my purpose that I should know exactly how matters stood between you and your husband."

Antonia moved slowly to a chair and sat down. She was calmer now, and conscious of the need to keep her wits about her.

"Your purpose being, of course, exactly what Sir Charles has believed all along? To possess yourself of his fortune?"

The faint smile broadened a little, but cold anger showed in his pale eyes. "A fortune which is ours by right. My father was Sir Charles's heir."

"Until Sir Charles had the impertinence to marry and beget a son!" Antonia's voice was scornful. "You speak as though he cheated you of your birthright by a trick. Do you know, cousin, I find that ridiculous?"

Roger's chair scraped suddenly across the floor as he rose abruptly to his feet; his lips were not smiling now and his eyes blazed. "Not more ridiculous than a man of three-and-forty losing his head over a girl not half his age! A pretty, silly creature with not even a respectable fortune to commend her! I was only twelve years old when Anthony was born, but I well remember the change it made in my life. As long as my father was Sir Charles's heir his credit was sound, but after that . . . !" He paused, controlling with an effort his unwonted betrayal of emotion. "This is a singularly pointless conversation, for you cannot be expected to appreciate the situation. Poverty, my dear Antonia, is one ill which you have never been obliged to bear."

She shrugged. "I have borne others." A frown creased her brow. "I can understand that you still covet Sir Charles's wealth even though you now have plenty of your own. What perplexes me is why you suppose that Geraint's death would help you to possession of it."

"That my son possessed it would be satisfaction enough. You were willing to marry Vincent before your grandfather forced St. Arvan upon you. I hope that, were you widowed, the match would still commend itself to you."

Her brows lifted. "Even if it did, do you suppose that Sir Charles would permit it, any more than he would before?"

"He could scarcely prevent it. You are of age now, and no longer a virtual prisoner in his house. Besides, you would be obliged to observe at least a year of mourning, and at your grandfather's age a year is a very long time."

She did not pretend to misunderstand him. "He cannot, I think, live so long, though he still clings obstinately to life, like a guttering candle which will not burn out. Even so, it seems to me that you are taking a great deal too much for granted. It is not only Sir Charles's consent which would be necessary. Suppose, after all, I were no longer willing to marry Vincent?"

He had resumed both his seat behind the desk and his air of faint amusement. "And *are* you willing, my dear?"

"That is scarcely the point," she countered after a slight hesitation. "In spite of your efforts, cousin, I still have a husband."

"Who is now convinced beyond all possibility of doubt that you have tried to bring about his death."

"That I have endeavoured it with your aid, sir. Now that I know the truth, what is to prevent me telling the whole story to Geraint, and so proving my innocence?"

"My dear Antonia!" Roger's tone was indulgent. "You cannot suppose that I would admit to St. Arvan, or to anyone else, what I have just, in confidence, admitted to you? There is not one shred of evidence which you could produce in support of such an accusation."

"No?" she said challengingly. "You have not carried out these murderous attempts single-handed. I would be exceedingly surprised, for example, to learn that it was you who laid in wait for Geraint on Finchley Common."

"Your surprise, child, would be justified. I was at White's that evening, and remained there until well into the early hours. The—er—other affair was carried out by my personal servant, Timothy Preston." He saw the startled expression in her eyes and smiled benignly. "Yes, my dear. The father of your abigail, Hannah, whom I was at some pains to introduce into your household."

The information shook her assurance a little, but she dissembled as best she might. "You repose singular confidence in your servants, sir."

"Ah, but Timothy is no ordinary servant! His father served mine; his mother was my nurse and Timothy and I were boys together. As soon as we were grown he entered my service. When I was obliged to leave England after the duel with your father, he came with me. He is wholly devoted to my interests and I trust him as myself. He *is* my second self."

"And his daughter?"

"Has been reared to accord me a similar loyalty, and has a wholesome fear of her father. You will not persuade her, either, to betray me."

Antonia had the sensation of a trap closing about her; one way out of it remained. "There is still Captain Bibury."

"Bibury?" Roger laughed gently. "No, my dear! He was hired—for I am sure you have realised by now that his supposed inheritance never existed—by a man whom I am willing to wager he could not now identify. This man represented himself as the emissary of a lady. A wealthy young lady who had been forced into a marriage repugnant to her, and wished most earnestly to be free of it. To achieve this she was prepared to pay very generously indeed. That, Antonia, is what Bibury will say if you are foolish enough to raise the alarm. It is what he believes to be the truth."

"But it was you who put into my head the notion of a duel between him and Geraint."

"You would have great difficulty in convincing anyone of that. I have been careful to let it be known that I viewed your flirtation with the deepest misgiving. I even suggested to my wife that she should drop a discreet word of warning in your ear. She did so, did she not?" Antonia nodded dismayed assent and Roger laughed again. "Precisely! I did not even make Bibury known to you in the first place. It was suggested to him that he should ingratiate himself with Letty Hurstwood, since no personable man ever experiences any difficulty in striking up an acquaintance with her, and the rest followed naturally enough."

So the trap was closed beyond any possibility of escape, though as yet she was not certain of his purpose in setting it. She only knew that she was afraid of this pleasant, smiling man as she had never been of her grandfather. Then, with the thought of Sir Charles, came hope, not of escape, but at least of a respite from a danger as yet only half understood.

"Geraint is not yet master of the Kelshall fortune," she said, and felt slight satisfaction because her voice was steady in spite of the pounding of her heart. "If I were suddenly widowed, I might well be just as suddenly disinherited."

He nodded. "I have been aware of that from the first, but the removal of St. Arvan seemed to me so urgent a necessity that I felt compelled to take the risk." He saw that she looked puzzled, and added with a touch of malice: "It would be an unwelcome complication, Antonia, if you were to bear a child."

She flushed, but said coldly: "With your spy in my house, sir, I am sure I do not need to tell you that there is now no possibility of an heir being born to the Kelshall fortune, so I am at a loss to understand your purpose in employing Captain Bibury."

"A natural impatience, my dear, to occupy the position I first aspired to more than twenty years ago," he replied smoothly. "You see, I have now devised a way of preventing Sir Charles from disinheriting you."

She laughed without amusement. "My dear sir, you cannot know my grandfather! While he has breath in his body he will do as he has always done—exactly as he pleases."

"Precisely! Therefore he will be made to believe that his best interests will be served by not disinheriting you. It is really very simple. When you are widowed, what could be more natural than for you to retire to Kelshall Park? When you arrive there, you will tell him that you are with child."

She stared at him. "You must be mad! How could I

maintain such a deception for more than a month or two? You have no means of knowing how long he may live."

"I think I have. Just now you likened his hold on life to a guttering candle which will not burn out, and so feeble a flame is easily extinguished. He need never know that you have deceived him."

Antonia felt a cold chill of fear closing about her. Geraint to be killed, and then Sir Charles, and then . . . ? Her mind shrank from the question but could not evade it. Would a man as ruthless as Roger Kelshall be content until he was undisputed master of the fortune which he regarded as his by right?

He was watching her intently, and with a tremendous effort she forced herself to appear composed. "I cannot believe you serious, cousin. You may be able to prevent me from exposing you, but there is no way in which you can compel me to take part in your vile schemes."

He did not immediately reply. For several seconds he pondered her, smiling, tapping the quizzing-glass thoughtfully against his chin, apparently not in the least put out by her defiance.

"But there is, my dear Antonia," he said gently at last. "You will take part in them because the alternative is so very unpleasant."

She looked distrustfully at him. "I do not understand."

"No?" He sighed. "It seems I have sadly overrated your intelligence. Permit me, then, to explain. Sooner or later, St. Arvan will die—by violence. You cannot prevent that, because even if you try to warn him, he now distrusts you so thoroughly that he will pay no heed. Once you are widowed, you will return to Kelshall Park, as I have described, and then, as soon as it is decently possible, you will marry Vincent. If you refuse to do these things"—he paused, and then added very deliberately—"you will find yourself on trial for the murder of your husband."

Antonia laid her hands on the arms of her chair and gripped hard on the gilded wood, fighting a sudden faintness. Through a mounting tide of darkness she heard Kelshall saying reflectively:

"There would be no doubt of your conviction. St. Arvan is already convinced of your guilt, and I have no doubt that Mountworth, at least, is in his confidence. Every particle of evidence points, and will continue to point, to you. Once the curious facts of your marriage and the even more curious facts of your parentage were made known, there is not a jury in the land which would acquit you. The trial and its—er—inevitable sequel would, I feel sure, create a sensation."

By sheer force of will Antonia conquered the weakness which had threatened to overwhelm her. "I marvel, then," she said faintly, "that you offer me any choice at all. Would it not be simpler just to let the Law take its course?"

"My dear child! You cannot suppose that I would involve us all in so unsavoury a scandal unless driven by the utmost necessity. Besides, there is Vincent to be thought of. He is devoted to you, and I would like to see him made happy. You need have no qualms where he is concerned. He knows nothing whatsoever of this matter."

"I never supposed, sir, that he did."

"No," Vincent's father agreed regretfully. "I fear he lacks both the resolution needful for such an enterprise and the worldliness to see where his best interests lie." He got up as he spoke and came round the desk to stand beside her, laying his hand on her shoulder. "But you do not, do you, Antonia? You see very clearly that you are completely at my mercy, and that the only course open to you is obedience. Implicit obedience in anything I may demand."

The touch of his hand on her shoulder was light, but to Antonia it felt already like the grip of an executioner.

Yes, God pity her, she could see. See the trap which, though Roger had sprung it upon her, had been forged out of her own folly and anger and hurt pride; see that she was snared fast in its murderous meshes, and that, no matter what her kinsman might say, her own danger, though less immediate, was as great as Geraint's.

Geraint, emerging alone from White's in the early hours, declined the porter's offer to call up a chair, waved away a sleepy link-boy who had started hopefully forward, and strolled off in a leisurely fashion in the direction of his home. The streets were deserted, for a heavy thunder-shower had driven any late wayfarers indoors, but now the sky was clearing and moonlight fitfully illuminated the way.

He sauntered along, carrying his cloak over his left arm and apparently enjoying the rain-freshened air, yet for all his seeming carelessness his senses were alert. For more than a week he had suspected that he was being followed. At first it had been no more than a vague, uneasy feeling of unseen eyes upon him. He grew more watchful and presently his suspicions were confirmed, though never in a manner definite enough to warrant any action. A shadow melting into the shadows of the night, a stealthy footfall behind him in a dark street, were all he had ever seen or heard of his pursuers, and yet he was certain that they were there, ready to fall upon him should a favourable opportunity occur. Tonight, he had decided, the opportunity should be offered.

At last his vigilance was rewarded by a slight sound a little way behind him. He swung round in time to see a man dart for shelter in a doorway, but since it was no part of his plan to let his pursuers know that he had seen them, he stood for a moment staring fixedly in the wrong direction and then with a shrug resumed his way, humming a snatch of song.

Apparently those who followed were not deceived, for they began to close in, with less regard now for stealth, and he heard the sound of at least two pairs of feet on the cobbles. Close at hand a side street joined the one he was traversing, and unhurriedly Geraint turned the corner; on his left a high wall was casting its shadow halfway across the street, and to this wall he set his back, at the same time drawing his sword. After a little while a man peered cautiously round the corner, and then, not perceiving his quarry, came right into the street, two companions at his heels.

"Behind you, my friends," Geraint said quietly. "You are seeking me, I think?"

The three swung round at the sound of his voice, checked for an instant at sight of the naked blade in his hand, and then circled warily about him, drawing their own weapons. The leader advanced, the swords met with a flash and flurry of steel, and at the same time the second man drove in a murderous thrust from the left, only to have his blade caught and tangled in the folds of the cloak. The third man hovered, awaiting an opening.

Geraint's point bit deep into the first man's shoulder, and with a howl the fellow dropped his sword and stumbled aside, the third darting forward to take his place. For a minute or so there was desperate work there in the moonlit street, with Geraint fighting for his life. A savage lunge was beaten aside only just in time, and the narrowness of the escape jerked an oath from his lips.

Footsteps pounded on the wet cobbles, a familiar and most welcome voice shouted encouragement, and Lord Mountworth flung himself round the corner and into the fray. Beset thus in the rear, one of Geraint's assailants uttered a cry of warning and took to his heels, while the other, obviously of greater hardihood, swung round to engage the newcomer. Leaving Peter to deal with him, Geraint sprang after the wounded leader, who was also endeavouring to retreat, and, gripping him by the arm, swung him about.

"Not so fast, my friend," he panted. "You and I have something to say to one another."

The fellow, with Geraint's sword-point at his throat, looked along the slim blade into the cold blue eyes beyond it, and thought it best to obey. Geraint jerked his head towards Mountworth and his adversary.

"Call off your henchman," he said shortly, "if you wish to save his skin and your own."

Once more his captive decided that resistance was useless, and called to his companion to yield. The order was obeyed reluctantly enough, and Peter possessed himself of his opponent's sword. Geraint addressed his own prisoner.

"Understand this," he said abruptly. "My quarrel is not with you. It is with the man who paid you to kill me, and if you will give evidence against him I will see to it that you both go free. I will even reward you."

The man leaned against the wall, clutching his injured shoulder, and nervously moistened his lips. "I'll tell you all I knows, sir," he said hurriedly, "but it ain't much. For one thing, I never saw 'er face . . ."

"What?" The word came like the crack of a whip, and Geraint's sword-point, which had sunk to the ground, leapt again to the speaker's throat. "Did you say '*her* face'?"

"That's right, sir!" The man shrank back and glanced uneasily at Mountworth. "A woman it were, a real gentry-mort, all silks and laces and powdered 'air—ah, and wi' jewels in 'er ears as would 'ave kept me in luxury for twelvemonth! I didn't see 'er face because she 'ad a mask on, but she were a tall, strapping wench wi' a 'aughty way o' speaking."

Geraint did not reply. As the man spoke he had lowered his sword again and now stood staring down unseeingly at the bright blade, his face very white. Peter cast a sharp glance at him and then said shortly:

"Where did you see this lady?"

The man named a tavern in a disreputable part of the city, and Mountworth said contemptuously:

"Do you expect us to believe that a lady of quality would ever know of such a place, much less venture herself there unprotected, wearing valuable jewels? You are lying, you rogue!"

"She weren't alone," the man replied sullenly. "There were a cove with 'er, a servant o' some sort by the look of 'im. Anyways, he were armed."

Geraint raised his head. "What was the man like?"

"I didn't see much of 'im neither, for 'e kept 'is 'at pulled well down, and 'ad a muffler round 'is face. Quiet-spoken, and not very tall. I didn't pay much 'eed to 'im, for I couldn't keep my eyes off them sparklers. Rubies, they was, an' diamonds. I see 'em when she put back 'er 'ood."

For a long moment Geraint continued to stare at the speaker, and then, with a gesture of resignation, he slowly returned his sword to its scabbard. "You can go," he said wearily. "Both of you."

Peter made a gesture of protest. "You cannot let them go free!"

"What else can I do? I cannot make use of such evidence as that. They can go to the devil, and the sooner the better."

Mountworth looked as though he were going to argue, but then shrugged helplessly and stepped aside. The two prisoners, awaiting no further invitation, made off as fast as they could, the injured man leaning for support on his companion.

Geraint picked up the cloak he had dropped and then

stood looking at it as though not quite certain how it had come into his hands. Peter gripped him by the shoulder.

"Let us go, Geraint," he said quietly. "There is no more to do here."

"So much for my scheme to trap Kelshall!" Geraint spoke with a bitterness Peter had never before heard in his voice. "Ironical, is it not, that I should risk my life to obtain information which I would infinitely prefer to be without?"

Mountworth made no reply, for there seemed to be nothing to say. They were sitting in the library of his house in Grosvenor Square, to which they had come after the fight, but though he felt that they ought to discuss the appalling discovery they had made, he found the subject singularly difficult to approach.

"Undoubtedly I am a fool," Geraint resumed after a moment, "but it never occurred to me that those fellows would lead me to anyone other than Kelshall. That is why I asked you to help me trap them."

"I suppose," Peter suggested hesitantly, "there can be no mistake? They never saw her face."

"There is no mistake. You heard what the rogue said. A tall, richly dressed woman with a haughty manner, wearing ruby and diamond ear-rings. Damn it, Peter! I gave her those gauds myself, when we first came to London."

"What about the man with her? Who could that be?"

Geraint frowned. "Certainly not Kelshall. Some creature of his, perhaps, but even if I could trace a connection it would not help. The fact remains that Antonia hired them. That is why the whole damnable affair must be kept secret."

Peter looked at him rather oddly. "I understand your feelings, of course," he said slowly, "but confound it, Geraint! This concerns your life. You cannot go on like this, never knowing when or where the next attempt will be made. One day they will catch you off guard."

"What, then, do you suggest?" Geraint got up and began to prowl restlessly about the room. "That I should have my wife arrested on a charge of attempted murder? Is that what you would do, if you were in my place, and Lucy in Antonia's?"

"That's no argument," Peter said impatiently. "Lucy and I . . ."

"Yes, I know!" Geraint broke in. "You love your wife. Well, I—God help me!—am fool enough to love mine. That is what makes it so damnably hard."

Once more Mountworth found himself at a loss for words. There was now no doubt that Antonia St. Arvan had cold-bloodedly planned her husband's murder, and though Peter's sympathy for his friend was profound, it was beyond his power to deny that fact.

"It is easy to be wise after the event," Geraint went on presently, "but I believe my mistake lay in bringing Antonia to London. If she had never become acquainted with Kelshall . . ."

"In my opinion," Peter put in bluntly, "your mistake lay in marrying her at all."

Geraint sighed. "Perhaps you are right," he admitted, "though I'll wager you would have done the same had such a choice been thrust upon you. No, I am convinced that Kelshall is the real power behind these attempts on my life. He wants Sir Charles' fortune for his son. That is why Vincent was sent to court Antonia in the first place."

"Well, if he hopes to secure a fortune for Vincent by marrying him to your widow, he is going about it in a singularly clumsy way. Deuce take it, Geraint! If they had killed you tonight, and the rogues had been caught, they would have led the Runners straight to your wife. She would have had no chance of escape."

"Do you think I do not realise it? Or that it makes my mind any easier? I would have thought Kelshall sufficiently shrewd to perceive it, too." He broke off, drawing a sudden, sharp breath. "Hell and the devil!"

Something in his voice and look brought Peter to his feet to grip him by the arm. "What is it?"

"Kelshall is no fool," Geraint said slowly, as though speaking his thoughts aloud. "We perceive the obvious. Depend upon it that he does likewise. If I am murdered, and information laid against my killers—which Kelshall could easily arrange—they in turn will betray Antonia. Thus every obstacle will be removed from his path, and he become complete master of the Kelshall fortune, which he will never be while she lives."

Peter was frowning. "If she were to marry his son, the fortune would be as good as his, for never tell me Vincent has spirit enough to defy his father."

"No, but Antonia has, as I'll wager Kelshall has discovered by now. I cannot imagine him tolerating such defiance. Oh, he is too damnably cunning! He must know that I would never take any action against her, and so even if things go awry, as they did tonight, he will be safe."

"It is possible that she perceives her danger."

"If she does, she has perceived it too late. She is so deeply implicated now that she cannot draw back even if she wishes to. Probably she does not. It is quite likely that her eagerness to be free of me blinds her to the peril in which she stands."

The bitterness was back in his voice, and Mountworth said quickly: "What do you mean to do? The situation cannot be left as it is."

"There is only one thing to do. Send Antonia out of London, so that if Kelshall wants to move against me he must do so himself, and I may find a way to turn the tables on him. She must go back to her grandfather. She'll not like it, but she will be out of harm's way there until I can settle matters with her kinsman."

Peter had gone to the window and flung back the long velvet curtains. The pale light of dawn was spreading across the sky, and in its greyness the candles in the room burned with a sickly light. He said over his shoulder:

"And if he makes no move against you? What then?"

Geraint shrugged. "Then I must force a quarrel on him and end the matter that way. I don't doubt I could do it."

Peter turned, frowning, to face him. "Wouldn't look well, Geraint. Confound it! The man's old enough to be your father. With your reputation, the consequences could be damned unpleasant."

"Less unpleasant than a knife in the back," Geraint retorted. "I should have to leave England, of course, but that would be no great matter."

"And your wife?"

Geraint threw himself into a chair again and looked up at his friend. His face was pale and drawn with something more than mere weariness, and the blue eyes had a haggard look.

"Yes," he said heavily, "my wife! That, my dear Peter, is a problem far less easy to solve."

Some hours later Antonia was sitting up in bed, sipping her morning chocolate and pondering, somewhat listlessly, the choice of a gown, when a peremptory rap fell upon the door. Hannah went to open it, and to Antonia's surprise Geraint came into the room and across to the bed, where he stood looking down at her with a decidedly forbidding expression.

The picture he contemplated so grimly was an agreeable one, for a beruffled wrapper of pale pink silk, and a lace nightcap tied beneath the chin with pink ribbons, became his wife extremely well, but appeared to have no softening effect upon him. He said curtly:

"You will be good enough, madam, to prepare for a journey. You will be leaving London at noon."

Her eyes widened in astonishment. "Leaving London?" she repeated. "Why, where are we going?"

His brows lifted, and there was a hint of mockery in his eyes. "I fear I must disappoint you, m'dear. *I* am staying in Town. You are going back to Gloucestershire."

She caught her breath, and her face paled until it was as white as the pillows behind her. She said with an effort: "My grandfather? Is he—has anything happened to him?"

"Not to my knowledge, for I have had no word from Kelshall Park. However, you will soon be able to allay your natural anxiety on that score." He turned to Hannah. "You will accompany your mistress. I expect her to be ready to leave by mid-day."

He was already on his way to the door when Antonia said desperately: "Geraint, I cannot leave London like this. I have engagements."

"Cancel them," he said shortly, and went out.

She gazed after him in stricken silence, and then looked at the servant. "But why?" she said. "Why?"

Hanah made no attempt to answer the question, but she drew near to the bed and said softly: "What's to be done now, ma'am? Had I best go to Mr. Kelshall?"

"Let me think!" Antonia pressed a hand to her forehead, for her brain seemed numb with shock and apprehension. "He must be told, I suppose, but help me to dress first."

While she was dressing, she tried to marshal her frightened thoughts. A return to Kelshall Park, at all times repugnant to her, had since Roger's sinister suggestion

concerning Sir Charles became fraught with danger. It
was true that he could not compel her to murder her
grandfather, but she had an uneasy feeling that Hannah
was unscrupulous enough to commit the crime, and Roger
sufficiently cunning to ensure that the blame fell upon his
cousin's shoulders. Her only hope, it seemed, lay in per-
suading Geraint to change his mind.

When she went downstairs she found with relief that he
was still in the house, waiting, she supposed, to make certain she obeyed him. She found him writing a letter, but
when she announced that she wished to speak to him he
laid aside his pen and replied, with cold politeness, that he
was entirely at her service. She thought, with an unexpected catch at her heart, that he looked older, and wondered wistfully if the seemingly irrepressible gaiety had
been banished for ever.

"Geraint," she said with as much composure as she
could muster, "why are you sending me away? Surely I
have a right to some explanation?"

For a moment or two he pondered her with hard eyes.
"We shall say, if you please, that your grandfather's
health gives cause for anxiety, and that you have gone to
him. That will prevent any curiosity, and provide you
with a reasonable excuse for breaking the engagements
you consider so important."

"No!" Her voice was sharp with alarm. "Do not say
that! If you must make some excuse, say that I have gone
for the sake of my own health, but do not mention Sir
Charles."

He frowned. "Why not?"

She was at a loss for an answer. It was impossible to
tell him that by doing so he would be playing into Roger's
hands, and no convincing falsehood occurred to her. She
turned away saying lamely:

"Never mind why. I would prefer you not to do it, that
is all. Besides"—she swung round again to face him—

"you have not yet told me your reason for sending me away."

"My dear Antonia," he replied in a level, ironical voice, "I am under no obligation to explain my actions to you. I have come to the conclusion that it is best for you to leave London. That it is best, in fact, for both of us."

"Best for both of us!" she repeated bitterly. "My God! You do not know what you are doing!" She caught him by the sleeve, sudden urgency in her voice. "Geraint, I beg of you, let me stay!"

He shook his head. "You are leaving immediately for Kelshall Park, so let us have no more argument on that score. No doubt you find it inconvenient to go into the country at this time, but console yourself with the reflection that your cousin will soon think of a way to amend any plans which my lack of consideration has overset. He is a far more able plotter than you are, Antonia, and you would do well to remember that. Now, by your leave, I will finish this letter to Sir Charles."

He turned back to the writing-table and, picking up the letter, began to read through what he had written. For a minute or two there was silence, while Antonia stood with her hands tightly clasped and her lower lip caught between her teeth, watching him with desperate eyes. At last her expression changed, and an air of strong resolution drove the hunted look from her face.

"I have something more to say," she said breathlessly. "You are right! I am privy to my cousin's schemes against your life, but only because he trapped me into it. I was so hurt and angry because you suspected me that, like a fool, I poured out the whole tale to him, never dreaming at that time that he had had any hand in the attack upon you. Then I met Captain Bibury—by chance, as I thought —and Cousin Roger told me he was the only man who might outmatch you as a swordsman. I wanted to punish you, to see you made a laughing-stock, so, to my shame,

I deliberately set out to provoke a quarrel between you and Bibury, but I swear I never meant to place you in any danger. My cousin said that only your vanity would suffer, and I believed him."

At her first words Geraint had looked up with an air of polite attention, and his expression did not alter. He said calmly:

"This confession comes a great deal too late. I am well aware of your conspiracies with Kelshall, and I fail to see what you hope to gain by this pretence of frankness."

"Oh, do you not understand? I have not conspired with him, not willingly. By my folly over Bibury I placed myself in my cousin's power, and now he believes that I fear him too much to defy him. Let him believe it! While he does, he will tell me what he intends, and if I stay in London I can warn you of any fresh plan he may make against you."

For an instant he looked blankly at her; then he laughed. "An ingenious plea, i'faith! Good God! Do you take me for a fool?"

"I mean it, Geraint," she said earnestly. "He is utterly ruthless, and nothing will stop him plotting against you. He will attempt your life again and again."

"Yet now *you* want to change sides," Geraint remarked, and added sharply: "Why?"

He expected her to tell him that she suspected Roger of treachery, and he was prepared to believe her. If she had realised the danger into which her plotting had led her, she would naturally try to escape from it, even if it meant joining forces with him. To his astonishment she made no mention of Kelshall. A tinge of colour crept into her white face and she said in a low voice:

"Because I have long since regretted trying to use Bibury to punish you—how bitterly I have regretted it! By doing so I increased your danger a hundredfold, and this is the only way I can think of to make amends. I did trick you into that duel, but, as God is my witness, that is the worst of my guilt. Believe that, Geraint, and accept the aid I am offering you."

She did not dare to look at him as she spoke, and so was unaware of the contempt deepening in his eyes. He watched her with a kind of amazement, marvelling at her effrontery, at the almost incredible treachery of this woman who could pay hired killers to murder him, yet at the same time, knowing nothing of his encounter with them, plead with him to trust her, offering to betray her confederate as proof of her good faith. Whose beauty still roused in him an agony of desire, and whom, cursing himself for his folly, he loved in spite of the evil he had discovered in her. He waited silently, wondering, with bitterness and disgust, how far she would carry this new attempt to deceive him.

"I realise now how blind I was," she continued. "How wickedly, wilfully blind! You were ill and feverish, and suspicion did seem to point at me. I should have been patient, waited until you were well again and could see how greatly you had misjudged me. I do not ask you to forgive me, for what I did is beyond forgiveness, but at least let me try to undo the harm."

"May I ask," he said expressionlessly, "how you propose to do that?"

"I have told you. As long as Cousin Roger believes me still in league with him, he will tell me what he intends. Thus you may not only defend yourself against his schemes, but even turn the tables upon him once and for all."

"And when Mr. Kelshall has been dealt with, what then? You say you do not seek forgiveness."

"I have no right to seek it," she faltered, "but if you wish me to plead for it, I will do so. Is that what you want, Geraint? To see me humbled, begging you to forgive me? See, then!" With a swift, graceful movement she flung herself on her knees before him, catching his unresponsive hands in hers; there was a sob in her voice. "Geraint, trust me, even if you cannot forgive! Ask any proof of my good faith and I will give it gladly, but do not send me away!"

There was a pause, during which she knelt there with bowed head, and then Geraint laughed, a soft, infinitely contemptuous sound that was like a blow in the face.

"Madam, you honour me beyond what I deserve. Into what trap do you seek to lure me now?"

Her head jerked up, her eyes incredulous, a dark tide of colour sweeping across throat and cheeks and brow. Geraint's expression was as contemptuous as his voice, and with a sob she covered her face with her hands.

"I am not as gullible as you seem to think," the hatefully scornful voice went on, "and if you and your cousin have laid a fresh snare for me, I suggest that you find some other means to entice me into it. These have been used once, and failed." He went to the door and opened it. "This is a singularly profitless discussion. Let us bring it to an end."

For a moment she did not move, but remained kneeling there with her face hidden. Then she rose and came with dragging steps towards him, but as she reached him she paused and looked up. He was watching her with cynical comprehension.

"*'Timeo Danaos'*, madam," he said, adding, as she stared blankly at him: "If my meaning is obscure, ask your kinsman to explain it. I feel sure that he is an excellent Latin scholar."

In Antonia's apartments a maidservant—not Hannah—was busy with trunks and bandboxes, and looked up nervously as her mistress came in, but Antonia did not even glance at her. She dropped into a chair and sat staring blindly before her, her hands lying limply in her lap.

She felt that she had plumbed the uttermost depths of humiliation, but neither that fact, nor the danger to herself which a return to Kelshall Park might involve, was foremost in her mind. During the past few minutes a truth had revealed itself to her, a truth so fundamental and overwhelming that it seemed incredible she could ever have doubted it. She still loved Geraint, loved him with all her heart. The fear and remorse which haunted her, her futile efforts to escape from the trap her kinsman had sprung upon her, had been prompted not by anxiety for her own safety, but for her husband's.

The bitterness of vain regret rose choking in her throat. There was no going back. It was even beyond her power to make amends, since, even though she had confessed her guilt and betrayed her accomplice, Geraint would not believe her. He meant everything in the world to her, yet she could not save his life.

For a while the horror of that thought possessed her mind, but gradually the old mood of rebellion awoke within her. It was not in her nature to submit tamely to despair; if it had been, her spirit would have been broken years before. There must be something she could do, something to save Geraint if not herself.

She found that she was staring at the servant packing her clothes, and this reminder of her imminent return to Kelshall Park reminded her also of one thing which she had until that moment forgotten. Geraint's only safeguard —and it was feeble enough—lay in the possibility that Sir Charles might disinherit her if she were suddenly widowed. As long as the old man lived that danger must be taken into consideration, but Antonia was now more than ever convinced that if she returned to Gloucestershire he would not be permitted to live long.

It was therefore imperative that she should escape from

her grandfather's house without delay, but to do that she would need help. There was only one person to whom she could turn. She hurried across to the escritoire and scribbled a hasty note to Vincent, but when she had sealed and addressed it she sat looking down at it in some indecision, wondering how to convey it to him secretly with all possible speed. Like most young men of fashion, he did not live at his father's house but in lodgings in a different part of town, so there was no danger of the note falling into Roger's hands, but if Geraint saw it he might possibly be moved to investigate its contents. At last she called the maid to her and showed her the letter.

"Do you think," she asked, "that you could find this address?"

With some difficulty the woman spelled out the name of the street, and nodded. "Oh yes, ma'am. I know where that is."

"Then take this letter there for me as soon as you can." Antonia produced some coins and put them, with the note, into the servant's hands. "Remember, I want no one to know of it."

"No, ma'am, and thank you." She stowed letter and money away in her pocket and permitted herself a small, conspiratorial smile. "You can trust me, ma'am."

Antonia sighed as she turned away. "I hope I can," she said under her breath. "More than one life may depend upon it."

Part Five

After Antonia's departure, Geraint sought forgetfulness in a round of dissipation which made his earlier excesses seem moderation itself by contrast, but nothing, neither gambling nor drinking nor the embraces of a mistress, could blot out the thought of Antonia's treachery. Until his encounter with her hirelings he had succeeded in convincing himself that Kelshall was the guiding spirit of the enterprise, and Antonia little more than a pawn in his hands, but now that comforting illusion had been shattered. She had gone herself to some thieves' den and bargained with men who lived in the very shadow of the gallows; she had set a pack of murderers baying at his heels, yet to serve her own ends had confessed with every appearance of remorse, and begged him to trust her. That was the measure of her hatred, and such venom was not provoked merely by the accusations of a sick man. She had hated him at the time of their marriage, and her feelings had never altered; betrayed by her own passionate nature into surrender, she had hated him even when, feigning love, she lay in his arms.

His reckless search for forgetfulness lasted a week. At

the end of that time his valet entered his bedchamber one morning, drew back the long draperies from the window, and then with some trepidation approached the curtained bed. His master, he found, had lately been of uncertain temper when roused, particularly when, as now, he had retired barely four hours before. Reluctantly he pulled aside the curtains, and as the daylight flooded in Geraint uttered a groan of anger and disgust and flung one arm across his eyes.

"Damn you to hell, Hinsham!" he said thickly. "What the devil do you mean by coming before I ring for you?"

"Your pardon, sir." Mr. Hinsham spoke apologetically. "I would not have ventured to disturb you, but a messenger has just arrived with a letter from Kelshall Park. He says it is urgent, sir. Extremely urgent."

"What?" Geraint raised himself on one elbow, gave an anguished groan and clapped his other hand to his head. After a moment he opened his eyes again to find that the valet was proffering the letter to him on a silver tray.

With an effort Geraint heaved himself into a sitting position, accepted the missive and broke the seal, observing as he did so that the letter was addressed to him in Edward Thornbury's writing. A glance at the first paragraph wrenched an oath from his lips, and he looked rapidly down the rest of the sheet. Then he read it through again, more slowly, and when he looked up, Hinsham saw that his eyes were no longer clouded, but hard and bright with anger.

"I am leaving immediately for Gloucestershire," Geraint said curtly. "Pack a change of linen and other necessities in my saddle-bags, and send word to the stables that I want the grey at the door in an hour. You will follow me with my luggage as fast as you can."

Hasten as he would, however, it was the following afternoon before he arrived at Kelshall Park, and when at last he swung out of the saddle in front of that forbidding mansion, there was a decidedly grim look in his eyes and about his mouth. He went quickly up the steps and into the house, and Edward Thornbury came hurrying to greet him.

"Has she been found?" Geraint asked abruptly.

The chaplain shook his head. "No, Mr. St. Arvan, not yet, though I have certain information . . ." He paused, and took the younger man by the arm. "Let us go into the library, and I will tell you."

In the library Geraint tossed hat and gloves on to a chair. The other man said solicitously.

"You must be in need of refreshment. Let me . . ."

"Nothing, I thank you," Geraint interrupted. "What of Antonia?"

Mr. Thornbury sighed and moved to the desk, which was covered with documents. As he began to gather them up he said slowly:

"Mrs. St. Arvan went riding each morning, alone. That had been her custom before her marriage, and not even Sir Charles saw anything suspicious in it. Even when, on the fourth day, her horse returned alone, our only thought was that she had met with some accident."

"As you were intended to believe! When did you discover your mistake?"

"Not until late that afternoon, when her maid found that all Mrs. St. Arvan's money and jewels had disappeared. Sir Charles realised then that she had run away, and sent to all the nearest inns and post-houses to find out if any vehicle had been hired . . ."

"Come to the point, man, for God's sake!" Geraint broke in impatiently, and strode forward to grip the other by the arm. "What the devil did you find out, that you are afraid to tell me?"

"Very well, sir." Mr. Thornbury lifted his mild blue gaze to his companion's face. "I am sorry to have to tell you that there can be no doubt your wife fled from here with the help, and in the company of, her cousin, Mr. Vincent Kelshall."

There was a pause. Geraint's grip on his arm slackened, and the chaplain saw a strange expression, a blend of bitterness and sorrow and pain, come into his face. It endured for a moment only, and then every other emotion was blotted out by a cold, deadly anger, and his hand went as though by instinct to the hilt of his sword.

"Did she, by God!" he said softly, and looked sharply at Thornbury. "How do you know?"

"A post-chaise was hired from the Blue Boar by a gentleman from London who spent two nights there. A slight young gentleman who spoke with a stammer. On the morning Mrs. St. Arvan disappeared the chaise was driven in this direction and later was seen passing through a village a few miles away, travelling towards Gloucester. There was a lady in the chaise, and a gentleman riding beside it."

Geraint nodded. "Kelshall, without a doubt! He must have followed her from London. What then?"

"That is all I know, sir. There has been . . ."

"All you know? Damnation, Thornbury, that was three days ago! Do you mean that inquiries have been carried no farther afield?" He checked, and added abruptly: "I will see Sir Charles, if you please."

"I fear, sir, that is impossible. Sir Charles . . ."

"One moment, Mr. Thornbury!" Geraint took him by the arm again; his voice was dangerously quiet. "Let us understand one another. I have no doubt that you are merely carrying out his orders, but I am not to be put off in this fashion. I will see Sir Charles if I have to force my way into his presence."

The little chaplain looked calmly up at him. "Sir Charles is dead, Mr. St. Arvan," he said quietly.

"Dead?" Geraint let go his arm and stared blankly at him. "When? Why was I not informed?"

"He died, sir, on the evening of the day Mrs. St. Arvan left this house. The news, of course, was sent to you at once, but you must have left London before it arrived. His anger against her was very great. He brooded over it all day, and when he found that it was Vincent Kelshall with whom she had fled he fell into a violent fury, cursing him, and her, and you, too, for not having kept a closer watch upon your wife. He was very weak, and the violence of his anger was too much for him. Those curses, I regret to say, were the last words he uttered."

Geraint turned away and went to stand by the window, looking across the gardens to the wooded hills. Sir Charles's death had long been expected, and it was impossible to mourn the passing of his crazed, tormented spirit, but the event had far-reaching implications. Kelshall was "Sir Roger" now, but the title was all that he inherited; Geraint himself was master of Kelshall Park and all the dead man's wealth.

"You will understand," Mr. Thornbury was saying, "that this melancholy event has made it impossible for me to pursue inquiries about Mrs. St. Arvan. I have been too much occupied with matters here."

"I understand perfectly, sir, and you have my gratitude." Geraint turned once more to face him. "*I* will carry out the search for my wife." He went to pull the bell-rope as he spoke. "I leave everything here in your charge, Mr. Thornbury, until I return."

The chaplain looked resigned, but said that he would discharge the trust to the best of his ability. A servant came in answer to Geraint's summons.

"I need a fresh horse—the best in the stables," St. Arvan informed him. "To the door in ten minutes."

"Mr. St. Arvan," Thornbury protested as the footman withdrew, "you have already travelled many miles. Surely you do not mean to set out again at once?"

"There are still several hours of daylight left," Geraint

replied shortly. "What is the name of the village where the chaise was last seen, and how do I reach it?"

The chaplain told him, but tried once more to persuade him to delay his departure until the morrow. Geraint turned on him with a kind of restrained savagery.

"Good God, sir! My wife has been in Kelshall's company these three days past. Do you expect me to idle here when I might be following them? Rest assured that I shall find them, no matter where they have hidden themselves."

"Mr. St. Arvan! Sir, I beg you to consider carefully what you do! When you find them . . . !"

Geraint was already at the door, but he turned and looked back at the chaplain. He smiled, yet there was death in his face.

"When I find them, Mr. Thornbury," he said quietly, "I shall kill him. This time he has given me every cause."

The trail of the runaways, already three days old, was not easy to follow. They had crossed the Severn at Gloucester and then turned southwards, and the pursuit grew steadily more difficult. Geraint rode that night until sheer weariness forced him to abandon the search, and was on the road again early next morning.

His progress was slow, for Vincent had been at some pains not to advertise his destination, and at every crossroads Geraint was faced with the risk of following the wrong path. Three times he had to retrace his steps by several miles, and finally, in a town of some size, lost track of his quarry completely. He spent the second night at an inn there, and on the following day, by a wearisome process of elimination, picked up the trail again, finding that it led him, by devious routes, out of Gloucestershire and deep into Wiltshire.

At last, late in the afternoon, he came to a tiny village, seemingly lost and forgotten in the depths of the lush countryside. By this time, alighting at the door of the one inn, he was tired and dusty and in a state of simmering fury, a hell's brew of anger and jealousy which had been seething within him all through these past, interminable days. He strode into the welcome coolness of the old, thatch-roofed house, calling impatiently for the host.

It was the mistress of the inn, a fat, placid woman whom nothing could fluster, who answered the summons. She brought him the ale he demanded, and listened patiently while he inquired whether a young lady and gentleman had halted there during the past few days; the lady tall and blackhaired, the gentleman with a slight stammer.

"Oh, you'll be meaning young Mr. Vincent, sir," she replied comfortably. "He didn't stop here, being so near the Manor, but my man saw him pass by. Riding beside a chaise, he was. I did hear as there was a lady with him. A cousin or some such, so 'tis said."

The stranger's lips tightened, and it seemed to her that a small flame leapt in the vivid eyes, but by contrast his voice was very quiet as he said:

"This gentleman—Mr. Vincent, as you call him. I gather you have seen him before?"

"Seen him before?" She shook with good-humoured laughter. "Why, bless me, sir! I've known him since he was in leading-strings, and a rare pretty child he was! Her ladyship fair doted on him—and does still, for all her sharp way of speaking."

Geraint was frowning. "Her ladyship? Whom do you mean?"

"Why, Lady Blackland, sir, to be sure! Mr. Vincent's grandmother. She brought him up, for his poor, sweet mother died when he was born. What with his father being so long in foreign parts, and then taking a second wife, he's lived nearly all his life at the Manor."

"One moment!" Geraint broke in. "I am not sure that I understand you. Do you mean to tell me that Vincent Kelshall has taken this lady—his cousin—to visit his grandmother?"

"Yes, sir, of course! Why shouldn't he? Her ladyship be main fond of company."

For some seconds he continued to stare at her, a curious expression in his face, and then he began to laugh as though he were both amused and angry. Gradually the amusement overcame the anger; he leaned his elbow on the table and covered his eyes with one hand, his broad shoulders shaking, while the hostess regarded him in perplexity. She enjoyed a laugh herself, but could think of nothing she might have said to provoke so much merriment.

He seemed to realise this, for after a little he raised his head, and she saw that the stern, angry look had gone from his face. "I laugh at myself," he said lightly, "and at what I have been imagining. I should have remembered that Cousin Vincent is nothing if not original."

The sun was sinking by the time Geraint rode up to the Manor, for he had stayed at the inn to dine, and to remove the dust of a day's travelling from his person. The house stood on a slight rise in the midst of a small park, a pleasant, rambling old building surrounded by well-kept gardens. When he sent in his name he was ushered at once into a white-panelled drawing-room of which the sole occupant was an old lady in a fashionable gown of stiff, violet-coloured silk. She was small, erect and exceedingly handsome, with abundant silver hair beneath a cap of delicate lace, and fine grey eyes very like her grandson's.

"Come in, Mr. St. Arvan," she greeted him affably. "I have been expecting you."

Geraint went forward, bowed over the hand extended to him, and glanced down at her with one eyebrow raised in quizzical mockery.

"I thought you might be," he said, "and I must apologise for my tardiness in arriving. I travelled here under a somewhat severe handicap."

The expressive, extraordinarily youthful eyes met his approvingly and with an unmistakable twinkle. She indicated a chair with a wave of her ebony cane.

"Pray sit down, sir." He did so, and she looked him over thoughtfully. "I must say, you are not at all what I expected."

"I believe I should be flattered," he replied with a quiver of laughter in his voice. "Your information probably came from a source prejudiced against me. I *am* correct, am I not, in assuming that you have been kind enough to extend hospitality to my wife?"

"You are, sir. She is walking in the garden, now that the heat of the day is over, with my companion and my grandson, but she will be here directly. Meanwhile, you and I may have a talk."

"Your ladyship is most kind. I should warn you, however, that my business here is chiefly with your grandson."

"You astonish me, sir," said her ladyship placidly. "May I be permitted to inquire what it is?"

"You may, madam, though I fancy there is no need. Mr. Kelshall is presumptuous. I have warned him, without effect, and so a sharper lesson is clearly indicated."

"I think not!" Lady Blackland rose to her feet and faced him squarely. "Understand this, Mr. St. Arvan! There will be no meeting between you and Vincent."

Geraint had risen also; there was a glint in his eyes. "I wonder," he said gently, "what makes you so certain?"

"I will tell you. You seem to me to be a man of sense"—Geraint bowed—"who would not wish to make a major scandal out of a very simple matter. Your wife ran away from her grandfather's house. That, I admit, was wrong of her, but I had some acquaintance with Charles Kelshall twenty years ago and I cannot find it in me to blame her. Vincent aided her in her flight, which was not only wrong but downright foolish, since he must have known that sooner or later you would find out. *But,* Mr. St. Arvan, he brought her to me that same day, and you do not, I trust, suspect *me* of subscribing to any impropriety?"

The laughter was back in Geraint's eyes as he looked down at the indomitable little figure. "Madam," he assured her solemnly, "I wouldn't dare."

"Fiddlesticks!" said her ladyship shortly. "I fancy there is very little you would not dare, young man, so don't lie to me. And don't tell me you are fool enough to think your wife cares for Vincent, for I'll not believe that either."

"I do not think it." He still spoke lightly, but now there was bitterness in his voice. "I am aware of something which Mr. Kelshall, perhaps, has yet to learn. That Antonia cares for no one but herself."

"Indeed?" She bestowed on him another of her wide, penetrating stares. "I should perhaps inform you that I am acquainted with the circumstances of your marriage."

"Then, madam, you should not be surprised to learn that it is a dismal failure."

"Nothing," her ladyship said caustically, "which concerns the folly of the young any longer has the power to surprise me." She returned to her chair and sat down. "Will you give me your word not to force a quarrel on Vincent? God bless my soul!" she added impatiently as he hesitated. "Do you think this story will ever become known unless you are foolish enough to make an issue of it?"

There was a pause. He was looking above and beyond her, out into the garden, and her own gaze rested thoughtfully and with a hint of anxiety upon his face. He seemed to be in the grip of conflicting emotions, for there was a frown between his brows and a certain grimness about the reckless lines of his mouth.

"Very well!" he said abruptly at length. "There will be no challenge on this occasion. If you value his safety, however, you will persuade him to hold aloof from my concerns in the future."

Lady Blackland smiled, and he reflected that she must have been extraordinarily beautiful in her youth.

"Thank you ," she said simply. "Vincent means a great deal to me."

"He owes a great deal to you, also," he replied with a touch of humour. "You have probably saved his life. I hope he profits by the lesson."

She shook her head. "You must not be too hard on him, sir. He sincerely believes that he loves Antonia."

"Does he?" Geraint's voice was suddenly hard. "Then I assure you that my sympathy for him is profound."

She raised her brows at that, and looked at him rather hard, but made no comment. Instead she rang the bell at her side, and when a servant came in answer to the summons she said: "As soon as Mrs. St. Arvan comes in, ask her to do me the favour of stepping in here. That is all you are to say. You understand?"

"May I ask why?" Geraint inquired when they were alone again.

Her ladyship chuckled. "A whim, Mr. St. Arvan. I am old enough to indulge in one occasionally. Well, now that you have found your runaway, what do you intend to do? You will, of course, be my guest for the present."

"You are too kind, madam. Will it not be less embarrassing for everyone if I withdraw to the inn in the village?"

"Not in the least," she retorted. "I have contrived to make your wife's visit to me appear the most natural thing in the world, and I do not intend to have all my efforts brought to nothing to spare your feelings, or hers, or Vincent's. My own do not enter into it. I shall certainly not be embarrassed."

He laughed. "In that case, Lady Blackland, I will accept your hospitality most gratefully—for one night. To-morrow I must return to Kelshall Park. Sir Charles died on the day of Antonia's flight, and though I have left matters for the present in the hands of his chaplain, there must be a great deal of business awaiting my attention. Antonia, of course, will go with me."

"Why 'of course'?"

He raised his brows. "I cannot leave her here."

"There is no reason why you should not. I have learned enough about her life at Kelshall Park to know that, whatever your differences, you should not compel her to return to that house at present."

"And Mr. Kelshall? I do not wish to imply that you are not a strict chaperone, but . . ."

"Vincent will be leaving for London tomorrow," she broke in to say with finality, "so you need have no uneasiness on that score." She leaned forward, speaking with the utmost seriousness. "Believe me, Mr. St. Arvan, it would be wrong—I might even say it would be cruel—to take Antonia back to Kelshall Park when she has known nothing but unhappiness there. Let her stay with me for the rest of the summer."

Geraint hesitated no longer. Lady Blackland's invitation was a heaven-sent solution to the problem, for he had viewed with considerable misgiving the prospect of taking Antonia back to Gloucestershire with him. The business arising out of Sir Charles's death was likely to keep him there for several weeks, and while sharing a house in London, where each had a busy social round to fill the days, was one thing, to be flung constantly into each other's company amid the isolation of Kelshall Park was quite another. With matters between them standing as they did at present, the situation would be intolerable.

"Your ladyship is most kind," he said, "and I accept that offer with gratitude. Whatever my wife may have led you to suppose, I have no wish to cause her needless distress."

Before she could reply, the sound of voices and footsteps outside heralded the return of the others. Geraint turned quickly towards the door, and her ladyship, after one swift, penetrating glance at him, looked expectantly in the same direction.

Antonia came unsuspectingly into the room, carrying a wide straw hat by its ribbons. She was wearing a very simple gown of white cambric over a slight hoop, and there were dark red roses at her breast. Geraint thought she had never looked more lovely. She stopped short with a gasp when she saw him, and for an instant, to Lady Blackland's percipient gaze at least, all heaven was in her eyes. The expression was gone in a flash, and apprehension and dismay rushed to take its place.

"Geraint!" she exclaimed in a small, breathless voice. "You here?"

His bow was formal. "As you see, madam. I appreciate your consternation."

Her ladyship looked from one to the other and rose to her feet. "You will have a deal to say to one another, no doubt," she remarked regretfully, "so I will leave you." She went to the door, which Geraint moved to open for her, adding as she did so: "It is always agreeable to know that one's suppositions are correct. Do not forget, sir, that I have your promise."

She went out. Geraint closed the door and turned to look again at his wife.

"Your promise?" she said uncertainly.

"Not to call Kelshall to account for his part in this affair." Geraint leaned his shoulders against the door and took out his snuff-box; his voice was contemptuous. "No doubt she is quite right. To blame him would be unjust, for I dare say you cajoled him into helping you."

She was trembling, and glad to lean on the back of a chair for support, but she managed to keep her voice steady enough to say:

"It *would* be unjust. Vincent merely escorted me here. You have no reason to call him out."

"Her ladyship has already convinced me of that." He took a pinch of snuff, closed the box with a snap, and returned it to his pocket. "Perhaps you will be good enough to explain why you felt yourself constrained to leave the house where I had placed you."

"I could not stay! I begged you not to send me there, but you would not listen." Her voice was shaking, and she paused to steady it. "Did my grandfather send for you?"

"No, Thornbury did. I regret to inform you that your grandfather is dead."

Her eyes widened. "Dead?" she whispered. "When? How?"

"On the day of your departure from Kelshall Park. As to the 'how' of it, it may be said that you were responsible."

He was unprepared for the effect his words had upon her. She took a pace forward, her lips parted, her face paper-white, and then, before he could make any move to save her, dropped fainting to the floor.

With a startled exclamation he went on one knee beside her, raising her with an arm beneath her shoulders, and at the same moment the door opened to admit Vincent, who came in with an air of resolution, saying:

"St. Arvan, I have just . . ." He broke off, staring. "Antonia! My God! What have you d-done to her?"

"Don't be a fool!" Geraint said shortly. He slid his other arm beneath her and stood up. "She has fainted, that is all."

"I'll f-fetch someone!" Vincent turned towards the door, but Geraint, looking down at the white face against his shoulder, said sharply:

"Wait! She is coming round. There is no need to cause a commotion."

He carried her across to the sofa, and as he laid her down on it she heaved a deep sigh and opened her eyes. Their glances met, and for a second or two it seemed that the gulf between them might be bridged, but Vincent, on the other side of the sofa, stammered an urgent question, and the precious moment was lost beyond recall.

"Antonia!" He caught her hand between his own. "Are you all right? What h-happened?"

With deliberate restraint Geraint placed a cushion beneath his wife's head and then stood upright, looking down from his superior height at the younger man. His eyes were brilliant with anger.

"Kelshall," he said with perilous courtesy, "your concern for your cousin does you credit, but I am more than a little weary of your interference in my affairs. Will you be good enough to take yourself and your damned impertinent curiosity elsewhere?"

Vincent was visibly shaken by this uncompromising demand, but he stood his ground and retained his hold on Antonia's hand. "I'll not go at your b-bidding," he retorted. "If Antonia wishes it . . ."

"Oh, go, for Heaven's sake!" she exclaimed, snatching her hand away. "Leave us alone!"

Vincent retreated in some disorder, and Geraint looked again at Antonia. She was watching him, her eyes enor-

mous in the pallor of her face, with some lingering terror
in their dark depths, and he bent over her in concern.

"I'm sorry," he said, more gently than he had yet spoken. "Had I realised how great a shock the news of Sir
Charles's death would be to you, I would have told you of
it less abruptly. Shall I find Lady Blackland and ask her
to come to you?"

She shook her head. "No, I am better now. Geraint!"
She sat up, clutching his sleeve in both hands. "What did
you mean—that *I* was responsible for his death?"

"It was an unfortunate choice of words, for which I ask
your pardon. Sir Charles was so incensed at the news of
your flight with Kelshall that he flew into a violent rage,
which in his weak state was too much for him. It was his
own dark passions which killed him, and not you or anyone else."

Her grip on his sleeve relaxed and she sank back,
trembling violently, her face still as white as the folds of
her gown. She looked frightened and forlorn, and he was
shaken by a sudden urgent desire to take her in his arms
and comfort her. Because the longing was so intense, and
the thought of her treachery towards him so bitter, he
straightened up abruptly and moved away from the sofa,
saying ironically:

"I do not know whether it is my arrival or the news of
your bereavement which has caused you so much distress,
or whether you merely dread being compelled to return to
Gloucestershire. If it is the latter, set your mind at rest.
Lady Blackland has been kind enough to offer you her
continued hospitality, which I have accepted on your behalf."

He did not look at her as he spoke, and so did not see
how her imploring glance followed him, or the little,
pleading gesture with which she stretched out her hand
towards him. After a moment the hand sank to her side,

and she said, in a voice which, though still unsteady, was
tolerably composed:

"Her ladyship's kindness knows no bounds, and I shall
be glad to stay, but what of you, Geraint? Are you going
back to London?"

"Not at present. I must first settle matters at Kelshall
Park."

"But when you do return to Town, you will permit me
to join you there? Oh, Geraint, I beg of you!"

He raised his brows. "To what purpose? Can you not
depend upon your kinsman to set you free, or is your
hatred of me so great that you *must* take an active part in
the business yourself?"

"How can I convince you?" she said despairingly. "My
purpose is to save your life. Your danger is much greater
now that my grandfather is dead, for only you stand between Cousin Roger and possession of Sir Charles's
wealth."

For a moment he contemplated her, scorn in his eyes.
"You convict yourself! Only I, you say, stand between
him and the fortune he covets, but, were I dead, that fortune would belong to you."

"He believes that I would marry Vincent and so place
control of it in his hands. If I refused, no doubt he would
kill me, too."

"Ah!" Geraint's tone was mocking. "At last we come
to the heart of the matter. You fear for your own safety."

"Believe that if you wish! Think what you will of me,
only trust me to help you!"

"Trust you? Gad's life, that's rich! Trust you, when you
have tried by every means you can contrive to bring
about my death?"

He turned to go, but she stumbled to her feet and,
reaching the door before him, set her back against it, bar-
ring his way.

"You shall listen to me! Do you not see that to go back to London alone is to play into his hands? It is not only he who threatens you. He will scheme and plan, but he will not attack you himself." She caught the front of his coat in both her hands; her words stumbled over each other in her eagerness to convince him. "He has a servant who is equally dangerous. Servant? 'Familiar' would be a better description. If the one is the brain to conceive a plot, the other is the hand to carry it out. I fear them both!"

Geraint listened without any change of expression to this breathless speech, and when she paused he said coldly:

"Will you have the goodness, Antonia, to stand aside? This argument is the same as that which we had in London, and as profitless. Let us bring it to an end, merely agreeing, out of deference to our hostess, to endeavor to be civil to one another while we are together beneath her roof. It will not be for long. I leave again in the morning." He paused, but when she did not move, took her by the shoulders and put her gently out of the way. "Then if you will not move at your own pleasure, you must move at mine, for I refuse to discuss this with you any further. You will remain here until I have settled my score with your kinsman. When that is done I will send for you, so that we may turn our attention to our own concerns, though God knows how we are ever to resolve that dilemma."

Geraint left the Manor early the next morning, but both his wife and his hostess were up in time to bid him goodbye. His parting from Antonia was brief and formal, but when he turned to take leave of Lady Blackland, she surprised him by saying:

"Take a turn in the garden with me before you go, Mr. St. Arvan. There is something I wish to say to you."

His brows lifted, but he agreed at once, proffering his arm to escort her out of the house and along a path which skirted the smooth expanse of lawn, across which the shadows of the trees lay long in the early sunlight. For a minute or two they strolled in silence, and then she said abruptly:

"I have no patience with people who pry into matters which do not concern them, but only a fool could be unaware of the fact that all is far from well between you and your wife. And I, Mr. St. Arvan, am not a fool."

"That, madam, is indisputable," he agreed with some amusement, "but, at risk of offending you, I must point out that this is a matter which I have no intention of discussing. You say you are aware of the circumstances of our marriage. That should be explanation enough."

"Fiddlesticks!" said her ladyship shortly. "Do not tell me, my dear boy, that it was beyond your power to reconcile Antonia to the marriage, for I shall not believe you. I fancy you would have contrived very well together had someone not interfered. Someone who considered it to be in his own interest to stir up trouble between you. Roger Kelshall, for instance."

Geraint cast a startled glance at her, and found that she was watching him shrewdly. After a moment or two he said carefully:

"I believe that Sir Roger does resent my marriage to his kinswoman."

"Resent it? Of course he resents it! Beware of him, St. Arvan! He is totally unscrupulous, and you could scarcely have a more dangerous enemy."

Once more Geraint paused before he replied. This turn of events was totally unexpected, and he was conscious of the need to feel his way cautiously.

"That is a strange thing to say, madam, of your own son-in-law."

"My son-in-law!" Lady Blackland's voice was bitter. They were in the shrubbery now, out of sight of the house, and she halted and turned to face him. "Roger Kelshall eloped with my daughter when she was barely seventeen. It was easy enough in those days to arrange a secret wedding, and for Phoebe's sake her father and I had to accept the marriage, though we knew well enough that Kelshall's only interest in her was her inheritance. He was less clever, however, than he had supposed, for Sir Arthur insisted that they live here with us, and kept a tight hand on the purse-strings. When Vincent was born, and Phoebe died, he made the child his sole heir. Vincent inherits when he reaches his twenty-fifth birthday in two years' time."

Geraint was frowning. "Then it was not for Vincent's sake that his father wished him to marry Antonia?"

"Roger Kelshall," said her ladyship tartly, "has never done anything for the sake of anyone but himself. Since Vincent went to live in London, his father's influence over him has become far greater than I care to see, and no doubt Kelshall believed that, if such a marriage could be contrived, it would give him virtual control of Antonia's money. He has coveted that fortune all his life. It is my belief—though I have never before admitted as much— that Sir Charles had good reason for his suspicions about his son's death."

Geraint was silent for a moment, looking down at her with narrowed eyes. "I wonder," he said slowly, "why you are admitting it to me?"

She shrugged. "I have lived long enough to know that time does not change a man of Kelshall's character. Twice he has seemed to have that fortune within his grasp, only to see it slip through his fingers, but he may still cherish hopes of Vincent marrying Antonia should any mischance befall you." She paused, and then added deliberately: "I understand that once already since your marriage you have come near to losing your life."

There was another, long pause. Geraint stood looking down at Lady Blackland, and her ladyship's expressive eyes met his with a wealth of meaning in their grey depths. Then he took her small, wrinkled hand and lifted it to his lips.

"I understand your ladyship, I believe, and I thank you for your warning. I, too, distrust Sir Roger Kelshall."

"Continue to do so, St. Arvan! He is a dangerous man. And have no anxiety about your wife. She will be safe in my care."

"I know it, madam, and for that, too, I thank you. I understand now why you were willing to befriend her."

"I like the girl," said her ladyship, with a sudden return to her usual manner, "and what is more, young man, I like you, but a more foolish, headstrong, wilfully undiscerning pair I have yet to meet. It is to be hoped that you come to your senses one day—though I place no dependence on it!"

Antonia remained with Lady Blackland for a month. Geraint made no attempt to communicate with her, and she knew that it would be useless to write to him. Hannah, who arrived at the Manor with her mistress's luggage a few days after his departure, could tell nothing beyond the bare facts of Sir Charles's death, and though Sir Roger must have learned from Vincent of her present whereabouts, no word came from him. At length, in desperation, she wrote to him, and received in answer a letter which told her, in guarded phrases, that nothing could be done until St. Arvan returned to London.

This brought a certain amount of comfort, for it

seemed that Geraint was safe for the time being, but, relieved of her most pressing anxiety, she now had leisure
to contemplate the extent of the rift between them. It was
too deep, she thought desolately, ever to be healed, and
though if he succeeded in getting the better of his enemy
he might choose to disregard the part his wife had played
in Kelshall's schemes, the memory of it must surely stand
between them ever after. They would never again find the
happiness which they had shared for so brief a time.

The peaceful interlude at the Manor was ended by the
arrival on the scene of Sir Roger himself. He arrived one
close, grey afternoon when the air was heavy with
thunder, glibly explaining his presence with a tale of a
visit to Bath, and a sudden decision to break his home-
ward journey in order to pay his respects to Lady Blackland and to offer her young guest, his cousin, condolences
on the death of her grandfather. Antonia was alarmed,
but, reading faint traces of strain in his face, and certain
that only the utmost urgency could have brought him to
the Manor at all, found enough courage, the first time
they were alone, to take him to task for the apparent in-
discretion.

"I did not look to see you here, cousin," she said with
a touch of malice. "Is it prudent, do you think, to single
me out in this fashion?"

"Prudence must sometimes bow to necessity," he said
curtly. "Did you know that St. Arvan is back in Town?"

"No." Antonia forced herself not to look up from the
embroidery with which she was engaged. "He has not
seen fit to inform me."

"That surprises you?" His brows lifted, and she
writhed in spirit at the mockery in his voice. "But then
you have not shown yourself to be a very devoted wife,
have you?" He paused, gently swinging his quizzing-glass
to and fro at the end of its ribbon, his gaze fixed on her
face. "May I ask if you are acquainted with the terms of

your grandfather's Will? No? Then it may interest you to know that, apart from certain bequests to his servants, Sir Charles left everything to St. Arvan. You, my child, have been virtually disinherited in favour of your husband, and must realise that, now Sir Charles is dead and the fortune his, St. Arvan no longer has any need of you."

He saw the little quiver of her lips as the deliberately cruel words struck home, and had time to appreciate a fleeting satisfaction. She set a few more stitches before she replied, though her hands were trembling so much that she could scarcely hold the needle, and then she said in a stifled voice:

"Need me or not, I am still his wife."

"Precisely, and so we have the interesting situation of a husband and wife, each equally anxious to be rid of the other, and yet with no way of accomplishing it save by violence."

"What?" Her caution swamped by a wave of horrified anger, she looked up to face him, wide-eyed and shaken. "You cannot think that Geraint would murder me?"

He shrugged expressively. "You have tried, have you not, to murder him? However, if that offends you, let us say instead that a fatal accident to you would cause him as little grief as you would feel for him in like circumstances."

She continued to stare at him, incredulous, yet gripped by a terrible doubt. "I cannot believe it!"

Roger shrugged. "Why not? Consider for a moment his unenviable position. Necessity forced him into a misalliance which has certainly brought him wealth, but which has also placed his life in constant danger. He is tied to a wife who is no wife. He knows that you have tried to bring about his death. Do you suppose that any consideration of loyalty or chivalry is likely to restrain him?"

A flash of genuine curiosity pierced her anguish. "Are you defending him, cousin?"

"I can appreciate his point of view, just as I can see that you would have been infinitely wiser to accept your marriage rather than to seek so earnestly to be free of it. Neither of these considerations, however, deter me from doing everything in my power to advance my own interests. That is why I am here. You must return at once to London."

She had already determined to do so, but thought it well to make some protest. It would only arouse his suspicion if she suddenly became too docile.

"If I do, he will probably send me away again. Why is my presence necessary?"

"Because with neither you nor Hannah in the house it is impossible for me to keep track of his movements. I dare not take the risk of introducing another servant of mine, even if there were anyone I could sufficiently trust."

"Very well!" Antonia spoke with a sudden air of decision. "When do you go back to London, sir? Will you give me your escort?"

His thin-lipped smile broadened. "With the greatest pleasure in the world, my dear. May I suggest—tomorrow?"

Lady Blackland, who had scented mischief from the moment Roger Kelshall drove up to her door, tried in every way she could think of to dissuade Antonia from going with him, but all her efforts were fruitless. Antonia set out with her kinsman next day, as he had known she would. He was very sure of himself.

They arrived in London at evening two days later. Sir Roger set Antonia and Hannah down in Brook Street, escorting his cousin to the front door, but declining to enter the house. A few moments later she was exceedingly glad that he had not done so, for as she went past the astonished servants who had admitted her she saw that Geraint was just coming down the stairs.

He was in full ball-dress, with a coat of sky-blue silk, satin small-clothes, and a lavishly embroidered waistcoat. His hair was powdered and dressed in formal curls, and there was a glint of jewels in the foam of lace which cascaded down his chest. At the foot of the stairs a lackey waited with his hat and silk-lined cloak.

At sight of his wife a frown gathered between his brows, but he neither checked nor hastened his leisurely descent. She paused in the middle of the hall and stood looking up at him, her dark eyes questioning and a little apprehensive, and for a few moments neither spoke. Geraint reached the foot of the stairs, strolled up to his wife and, taking her hand, bent to brush it with his lips.

"This is an unexpected pleasure, m'dear," he said amiably. "You should have sent word of your coming."

He had retained his clasp on her hand as he spoke, and now drew it through the crook of his arm and led her into the library at the back of the house. As soon as the door was closed and they were alone, his manner changed abruptly. He released her and said sternly:

"Why have you come back?"

"Why should I not?" She moved away from him into the room, drawing off her gloves. "You surely did not expect me to stay with Lady Blackland forever?"

"I expect you to do as I bid you," he replied angrily. "When I left you at the Manor I told you to remain there until I had settled matters with your kinsman, which I have not yet done. No doubt I have him to thank for this most inopportune arrival."

"Inopportune!" She gave a short, angry laugh. "Faith, you are frank!"

"I will be franker yet. Keep out of Kelshall's schemes in future, or you will regret it. Whichever way the affair

ends, there is likely to be a very pretty scandal at the
last." He turned again to the door, but paused to say over
his shoulder: "Have the goodness to remember that you
are in mourning, and cannot attend any social functions."

He went out. She heard his voice addressing some remark to the servant, and then the closing of the front
door, and wondered miserably whom he was going with
such eager haste to meet.

It was on the following morning that Antonia decided that
she would have to kill Roger Kelshall. The idea came to
her quite suddenly, after a sleepless night spent racking
her brain for some way of convincing Geraint that her
desire to help him was genuine, or, failing that, of preventing Sir Roger from carrying out his deadly design.
The one seemed as impossible to accomplish as the other,
for Geraint would not even listen to her, and Sir Roger
would be a menace to him as long as he lived.

As long as he lived. Antonia sat very still, wondering
why so simple a solution had never before occurred to
her. Roger first, and then herself. She even had the means
to do it. The little, antique dagger with which she had
once threatened Geraint, and which lay now in a locked
drawer in her dressing-room. In that sharp, bright blade
lay the answer to all her problems.

All that remained was to find an excuse to call upon
him, and that luck favoured her at last. Lucy Mountworth, who had met Geraint the previous night and
learned of Antonia's return, came to call, greeting her
friend with pleasure mixed with a curiosity she was too
well-bred to indulge, and sympathising with her because
mourning precluded her from attending any parties. Lucy
herself, it seemed, was taking a party of friends to a masquerade at Vauxhall Gardens the following evening. Ger-

aint had already accepted an invitation, and it would have been so delightful if Antonia could have come, too.

Antonia replied somewhat at random, and as soon as Lucy had gone, summoned her carriage to take her to Sir Roger's house. On the way she pondered, almost indifferently, the interpretation the world would put upon her deed. Probably they would say that she was mad. That was the verdict most often brought in cases of suicide; the only one which made it possible for the guilty person to be given Christian burial. Only Geraint, perhaps, might guess something of the truth, and know at last that she had been sincere in her desire to save him.

Though her mind was acutely calm and clear she felt that she was moving in a dream, in which the only reality was the dagger concealed in her feather muff. When she reached Kelshall's house she told the butler that she had urgent private business with Sir Roger, and in a very few minutes was ushered into the study. Roger rose from the big desk to greet her, taking in both his own the hand she put out to him.

"My dear child, this is a charming surprise! I did not expect to see you again so soon. Come, sit down!"

She sank into the chair he indicated. "I have news that will interest you, cousin," she said, doing her best to speak naturally. "Geraint goes to Vauxhall tomorrow night, to the masquerade."

He had seated himself at the desk again, and he continued to watch her as though expecting something more. At length he said questioningly: "Well, my dear?"

"Well?" she repeated impatiently. "Is that all you have to say, sir? I thought you desired me to return to London so that I could keep you informed of his comings and goings?"

"Precisely, but I wonder why you have chosen to bring me this particular piece of information."

A tiny shadow of uneasiness began to take shape at the

back of her mind, but she forced herself to make a show
of impatience and even of anger.

"Lud, man! Is this not the opportunity we have been
waiting for? You know the gardens! Those shadowy walks
and little summer-houses might have been designed for
our purpose, and tomorrow night they will be thronged
with people in dominoes and masks. What could be better?"

"What, indeed?" he repeated thoughtfully. "Dominoes
and masks! Precisely! Of course, it may be a trifle difficult to locate our quarry, since he will share the general
anonymity."

"I will make it my business to find out how he will be
dressed. If necessary, I will even go to Vauxhall myself."

"You are very eager, my dear. May I inquire the reason for your sudden bloodthirstiness?"

"Need you ask?" Antonia got up and began to move
about the room as though her feelings were too violent
for her to remain still. "Can you not imagine the reception I got yesterday? The manner in which I was berated
for having dared to disobey him? I am to go back to Kelshall Park, he says, and remain there in the care of Mr.
Thornbury and the servants. I am to be a prisoner, in
fact! I tell you, cousin, I am weary to death of being
threatened and humiliated!" She was standing just behind
him now where he still sat at the desk, and inside the
muff her fingers curved tightly round the hilt of the dagger. "If the thing is to be done, in God's name let it be
done soon!"

As she spoke she slid the knife out of its sheath, her
gaze fixed on Kelshall's back. He was sitting with his head
slightly bent and his hands resting lightly against the edge
of the desk; he had made no move to turn and look at
her. "For your sake, my love," she thought as her hand
clutching the dagger came out of the muff, and struck
downwards with all her strength.

At the same instant, as though aware of her intention, Sir Roger flung himself sideways out of his chair, and the knife, hard-driven, bit instead into the wood of his desk. Before she could wrench it free he was on his feet, gripping her in ruthless hands, while the big mirror on the wall facing the desk swung open like a door and Timothy Preston burst into the room.

One glance was sufficient to show him what had happened, and he hurried across to them. Roger handed over his captive and the servant took her in a practised grip, twisting her arm up behind her back in a way which put a speedy end to her struggles.

Kelshall picked up the fallen chair, and settled his coat and straightened his cravat in a leisurely, unhurried way. Then he took up the dagger and ran a reflective finger over the gash it had scored in the desk.

"Extremely annoying, Timothy!" he remarked. "We shall now be obliged to think of a story to account for this. Antonia, my dear, you are really quite troublesome—and extraordinarily careless. You should have remembered the mirror."

She caught her breath, and followed his glance across the room. Roger's thin lips curled sardonically.

"Precisely!" he said softly. "I had the privilege of watching every move you made, although I confess I was already made suspicious by your sudden eagerness to be widowed. Were you really foolish enough to suppose I did not know that you would go to any lengths to save your worthless husband?"

He put the dagger down and quite dispassionately struck her twice across the face, first on one cheek and then on the other. Then he nodded to Preston.

"Let her go," he said. "She will give us no further trouble. Sit down!" he added to Antonia.

She sank into the nearest chair, too shaken to protest, too horrified by her failure and her self-betrayal even to feel resentment of the blows. Kelshall also resumed his seat and once more took up the dagger.

"A useful weapon," he commented, cautiously testing the blade with his finger, "but scarcely safe in such impetuous hands. I think I had best keep it for the present. There should be a sheath of some kind. Ah, Timothy, I believe you will find it in Mrs. St. Arvan's muff, which we have so carelessly left lying on the floor. Thank you! No, you may return the muff to her—and, Timothy, I desire you to remain in this room. You may sit down."

Antonia was rubbing the arm which Preston had so cruelly twisted, but at that she said with a touch of defiance: "Do you think, cousin, that you need protection?"

He shook his head, smiling at her with the utmost goodwill. "Not in the least," he replied pleasantly. "You, I fancy, have shot your bolt. Now let us turn our attention to the trap we are to lay for St. Arvan tomorrow night."

She stopped rubbing her arm to stare at him in stupefaction, while even Timothy Preston looked startled. At last Antonia found her voice.

"You must be mad," she said bluntly.

"I think not, my child. In fact, I find your suggestion admirable. A masquerade at Vauxhall! Yes, I like the notion very much."

She made an impatient movement. "You know very well I used that simply as an excuse to come here."

"Yet St. Arvan *is* going to Vauxhall?"

"Yes, with the Mountworths, but nothing in the world will persuade me to aid you in harming him. I'll plot with you no more!"

"I am afraid, my dear Antonia, that you have no choice."

"Have I not?" Her chin was up, her eyes blazing defiance. "I can always give myself up to the Law, and confess everything. I no longer care what befalls me, as long as you come by your just deserts."

"No doubt, but, you see, I would not come by them. There is not one shred of evidence to support your accusations, for I should naturally deny everything, and so would Timothy and Hannah. On the other hand, there is a great deal of evidence that you have tried to have your husband murdered. Even St. Arvan himself believes it. You would simply destroy yourself without harming me or saving him, for do not flatter yourself that I would desist simply because I was deprived of your assistance."

He paused, leaning back in his chair with his elbows on the arms and the tips of his fingers pressed lightly together, and steadily regarded her. His expression was indulgent, but the pale eyes were utterly merciless and she realised, with sudden fearful certainty, that there was no escape for her. The only hope that remained was to pretend acquiescence in whatever he planned for the following night, and to try to warn Geraint of the trap. Roger, for all his vaunted cleverness, had overlooked that possibility.

"I suppose I shall have to help you," she said sullenly. "What do you want me to do?"

Sir Roger beamed his approval. "I felt sure that you would see the wisdom of agreeing," he commended her. "I shall be obliged to give the matter some thought, but by tomorrow evening I shall undoubtedly have hit upon a plan. Have your coach set you down at Westminster Bridge Stairs at ten o'clock. I will be waiting for you there."

She shrugged. "As you please, but I cannot go to a masquerade without a domino, and I have none. If I try to obtain one it is likely to come to Geraint's ears. Do not forget that I am supposed to be in mourning."

"I will provide you with domino and mask. Send Hannah to me as soon as you return home, and it shall be arranged. Now you had better go, for we do not wish to

arouse suspicion by being too long together. Let me conduct you to your carriage."

When Sir Roger returned alone to the study he was
rubbing his hands and looking exceedingly pleased with
himself, but Preston did not appear to share his satisfaction. He was standing by the desk, examining Antonia's
dagger and frowning.

"Well, Tim?" Kelshall greeted him. "Why that mourn-
ful face?"

Preston shook his head. "I don't like it, sir," he said
positively. "She agreed too readily. I'll stake my life she
means mischief."

Sir Roger shrugged. "What can she do? She has no
proof of our bargain. No proof, even, that I desire St. Arvan's death."

"Sir Roger, if Mrs. St. Arvan goes to Vauxhall tomorrow night it will be for one purpose only—to warn her
husband."

"Of course. Did you think me unaware of that?"

"Then why, sir, in God's name?"

Kelshall sat down at the desk and leaned his arms upon
it, contemplating his servant with an ironical expression.
"Come now, Tim, you should not need me to point out
the obvious. Unless Antonia is at Vauxhall, how can I
make certain that blame for the crime will fall upon her?"

Part Six

At nine o'clock on the following evening Antonia was seated at her dressing-table. Though she still wore a loose powdering-gown over her underdress of ivory-coloured satin, her hair was already dressed and heavily powdered. Hannah hovered attentively round her.

"Mr. St. Arvan went off early to dine at Lord Mountworth's," the abigail volunteered, handing her mistress the patch-box. "He was wearing the peach-coloured velvet, with a flowered waistcoat, and carrying a grey domino."

Antonia's fingers trembled as she pressed a tiny round of black silk on to her cheek. Hoping that Hannah would not notice, she said petulantly: "Grey, was it? There will be scores of grey dominoes, I have no doubt."

"Pearl-grey," Hannah offered helpfully. "Do you think you'll be able to find him?"

"I trust so." Antonia compressed her lips, for there was a new insolence in the girl's manner. She was respectful enough when anyone else was present, but when they were alone she treated her mistress as an equal. "Did my cousin give you a domino for me?"

"Yes." Hannah lifted the lid of a band-box which

stood on a nearby chair and took out a domino of scarlet silk. Antonia stared in dismay as the voluminous folds, brilliant as a poppy's petals, cascaded over box and chair alike.

"Heavens!" she exclaimed. "I cannot wear that! I am supposed to be in mourning."

"If you're in mourning, you shouldn't be at a masquerade at all," Hannah pointed out reasonably. "No one will know who you are. See, there's a mask as well. You'll never be recognised in that."

Antonia took the mask held out to her. It was of the same vivid silk as the cloak, and there was a deep frill of lace of the same colour, scattered with tiny gems, hanging from its lower edge. When she held it in place, it concealed her face almost to the chin.

"I suppose you are right," she said reluctantly, "but I do think he might have chosen something less conspicuous. I do not suppose there will be another domino of just that colour in the whole Gardens."

Hannah was quite sure there would not, for she had had a great deal of trouble to procure that distinctive hue, and she knew that her purchase of the conspicuous garment on Mrs. St. Arvan's behalf, and her insistence that the transaction be kept secret, had caused more than a little speculation. She said soothingly:

"I fancy Sir Roger wants to be sure of finding you in the crowd, and there's one thing—St. Arvan would never suspect you of going to the masquerade in such a striking dress when you are supposed to be at home."

Antonia was not entirely convinced, but it was too late to make any change. She rose to her feet, tossed aside the powdering-gown and allowed the abigail to put her into an overdress of ivory brocade, and lace it up. As she tugged and patted it into place, Hannah said:

"You'll wear the ruby and diamond ear-rings, I dare

say? I've put them out for you. Oh, and Sir Roger sent the white roses, and asked particularly that you should wear them."

"Oh, very well," Antonia glanced at the clock, "but hurry, for pity's sake. I am to meet him at ten."

A few minutes later, with rubies and diamonds glittering in her ears, the domino over her arm and the mask dangling from one hand, she went quickly down the stairs and out to her coach. Hannah, watching from the first landing, saw the footman cast a startled glance at the folds of scarlet silk, and smiled to herself. Sir Roger was right; that colour could not fail to attract attention.

Kelshall had a boat waiting when Antonia arrived at Westminster Bridge Stairs, and handed her into it without delay. He was already masked and wearing a black domino flung back from his shoulders, and she was glad that some instinct of caution had prompted her to don her own mask in the coach. She had been prompted as much by the desire to hide her face from his shrewd gaze as by the fear of being recognised, but she soon realised that they were not the only revellers who had chosen to go by river to Vauxhall, and though she saw no one she knew she was thankful that her features were concealed.

He had taken care to greet her with commonplace civilities suitable to the occasion, but once they were under way and being rowed briskly upstream, he said in a voice too low to reach the ears of the watermen:

"Do you think you will be able to find St. Arvan among the crowd?"

Antonia nodded. She felt certain that she would recognise Geraint anywhere and at any time, were he never so closely disguised; it was impossible, she thought, that she could ever be unaware of his presence. Aloud she said:

"Oh yes, I think so. Mountworth's party should not be difficult to discover, and I know how he is dressed, but what am I to do when I have found him? Have you a plan?"

"Of course. When you have found him, keep him in sight, and as soon as you can do so unobtrusively, approach and speak to him."

"Speak to him?" she repeated blankly. "But if he knows I am at Vauxhall he will make me go home again."

"Heaven grant me patience! You will not, of course, disclose your identity. These Vauxhall masquerades are not altogether genteel, you know, and it is by no means uncommon for a female of a certain class to approach a gentleman. If you play your part convincingly he will not suspect you."

In the shadow of the lace-trimmed mask Antonia's lips tightened. His voice was mocking, and she knew it amused him to suggest that she should assume the manner of a harlot and accost her own husband. She would have liked to refuse, but the opportunity thus offered her to warn Geraint of his danger was too precious to cast away.

"You flatter me, cousin," she said dryly. "What then?"

"You will make an assignation with him, for midnight, at the entrance to the card-room. Then you will persuade him to accept one of those roses you are wearing, and fasten it in his coat."

"And after that?"

Sir Roger looked at her, and below his mask she could see that a mocking smile was curving his lips. "That, my child, I will tell you after you have made the assignation. Just as a precaution, you know. I am sure you appreciate the necessity. Now, do you understand what you have to do?"

"I understand," she said quietly, "and I will not fail. Too much is at stake."

When they reached the entrance to the Gardens, and the boat drew alongside the landing-stage, a slight man in a black mask and domino stepped forward to offer her his hand. She hesitated, glancing questioningly at Sir Roger, who smiled and nodded.

"It is Timothy," he said in explanation. "I told him to meet us here."

Anotonia accepted the proffered assistance, and stepped ashore. Sir Roger, following, put the scarlet domino about her shoulders.

"Fasten it," he said briefly. "He may recognise your gown."

He waited until she had tied the strings, then, drawing her hand through his arm, and signing to Timothy to walk on her other side, led the way towards the centre of the Gardens.

"I shall leave you in a moment," he informed her as they strolled along, "but you will be quite safe in Timothy's care. Try to find St. Arvan without delay. I advise you to inspect the boxes first, for he may be at supper. Tim, you know when and where we are next to meet."

He bowed and left them, and Antonia walked on with Preston. It was a beautiful night, warm and still, and the Gardens looked their best in the light of a full moon and of the hundreds of lamps with which they were decorated. Muisc floated softly on the air, and beneath the trees, whose leaves hung motionless against the deep blue sky, crowds in dominoes of every imaginable colour were strolling about, laughing, gossiping and flirting.

It was a gay scene and one which had never before failed to delight her, but tonight she viewed it with different eyes, and found it horribly macabre. The laughter grated upon her ears, the gaily clad figures whose eyes glittered so strangely through the slits of their masks were phantoms in a nightmare world. Though none of the revellers knew it, murder was abroad, stalking in mask and domino through their lighthearted ranks, seeking its victim.

When they reached the open space where the two semi-circles of boxes faced each other, she realised for the first time the magnitude of the task she had set herself. In almost every booth parties of varying sizes were at supper, while in the space between crowds of people were moving to and fro. Within a minute she had seen no less than three grey dominoes, and though none of them could conceivably be worn by Geraint her heart sank at the prospect before her.

The succeeding minutes did nothing to raise her hopes. On Preston's arm she paced slowly around the line of boxes, anxiously scanning their occupants, and the people among whom she moved. Grey dominoes there were in plenty—slate-grey, steel-grey, dove-grey and pearl-grey. To Antonia's bewildered and despairing eyes it seemed that the entire Gardens were peopled with gentlemen wearing that particular colour.

She had halted close to the front of one of the boxes, and was peering to see whether a tall Grey Domino who had just passed was wearing peach-coloured velvet beneath his cloak, when an unmistakably familiar voice spoke just behind her.

"Mountworth!" said Lucy, in what she no doubt thought was a discreet whisper. "Only look at that scarlet domino. Is it not enchanting? I have never seen such a colour."

Antonia started violently, her hand tightened involuntarily on Preston's arm, and only by a supreme effort of will did she refrain from swinging round. Lucy's voice had come from the box beside her, which had been empty a moment ago, and so Mountworth's party must just have entered it through the door at the rear. She forced herself to walk on, and to wait until a discreet distance intervened before she ventured to look round.

There were six people in the box. Lucy, in blue, was

easily identified by the jewels she was wearing; Geraint stood beside her, one hand resting on the back of her chair as he addressed some remark to a gentleman in crimson whom Antonia guessed to be Lord Mountworth. The other three people, two ladies and a gentleman, she could not identify.

"You have seen him?" Timothy asked softly.

She nodded. "In the third booth from the left. They are just sitting down to supper."

"Excellent!" Timothy said in satisfied tones. "In that case, madam, may I suggest that we do the same? There is a box vacant yonder from which we may watch them without drawing attention upon ourselves."

She agreed with relief. It was obvious that she could not approach Geraint until his party left their box, and she felt that she would be glad to remove herself from the prominent position she now occupied. Lucy's comment on her attire was by no means the only one she had heard, and many heads had turned as the Scarlet Domino passed by.

Once seated in the shelter of the booth she felt more comfortable, though even then she was not entirely safe from curious eyes. A rakish gentleman in violet ogled her in a determined fashion from a neighboring box, and once she suffered an unpleasant qualm when, glancing towards Mountworth's party, she found that her husband was critically studying her through a levelled quizzing-glass. She drew farther back into the shadows, averting her face and lifting a nervous hand to her mask. When she dared to look in his direction again, he was engaged in conversation with one of his companions.

At last, after an interminable interval, Mountworth's party rose to leave their box. Antonia and Preston followed suit, and after a few uneasy moments when it seemed that they had lost track of their quarry, discovered them making their way towards the pavilion, where dancing and gaming were in progress. As she and Timothy drew near, Antonia indicated a seat at the side of the path.

"Wait for me there," she whispered. "It will not do for me to have an escort with me when I speak to him."

She half expected some argument, an insistence that he should at least remain within earshot, but to her relief he agreed to her suggestion at once. She left him thankfully; so thankfully, in fact, that it never occurred to her to wonder why Sir Roger's henchman should be so accommodating.

Geraint, sunk in a momentary fit of abstraction, was startled out of it by the touch of a hand on his arm. He halted and looked round, to find himself face to face with the Scarlet Domino whom he had noticed earlier. While he stared at her in surprise, she said in a breathless, husky voice:

"Sir, will you walk with a me a little? I would like to talk to you."

Surprised, amused, even a little suspicious, he continued closely to regard her, and then suddenly his eyes narrowed. The red mask with its deep frill of lace effectively concealed her features, but as she turned her head to cast an anxious glance after his companions, a ruby and diamond ear-ring glittered in the light of a nearby lamp. A grim little smile touched his lips.

"With the greatest pleasure in the world, m'dear. Where do you suggest we go?"

"This way." The hand on his arm tightened, and she drew him towards that secluded path known as the Lovers' Walk. "It is necessary that we are not observed."

Warily, half expecting to be led into an ambush of

some kind, he followed her into the shadows. She led him on without speaking until they reached a remote corner, then, turning to face him, stripped off her mask. His brows lifted a little, but otherwise he made no response.

"Well?" she said challengingly after a moment. "Are you not surprised?"

He shook his head. "No," he replied apologetically. "You see, m'dear, I recognised you when you spoke to me. These trinkets"—he flicked one ear-ring lightly with his finger—"gave you away. It was careless of you to wear them."

"Oh!" Her own hand flew up to touch the ornament. "I had forgotten them, but it does not matter. Geraint, you are in danger here!"

"That I suspected." He glanced to right and left. "Why do your cut-throats not spring out upon me? I must warn you, however, that I shall make a determined effort to defend myself, and the noise of a fracas is likely to attract attention. Do you not think that perhaps it would be wiser to postpone my demise?"

"Ah, must you be jesting still? I am trying to warn you of the trap, not lead you into it. My kinsman is somewhere in the Gardens, and his servant also. Oh, trust me, for pity's sake!"

There was a frown in Geraint's eyes. "If you wanted to warn me, why did you not do so before I left the house?"

"Because I do not yet know what Cousin Roger is planning. I am to make an assignation with you outside the card-room at midnight, and until that is done he will not tell me what he intends. He knows I would betray him if I could, but believes he has sufficient hold over me to make me obey him."

"Outside the card-room?" Geraint was sceptical. "You are not asking me to believe they'll set upon me there?"

"No, of course not. I imagine the plan is for me to lead

you to some quiet spot where they can attack you. Oh, Geraint, go before they realise I have warned you! You can make some excuse to Lucy."

"And when I fail to keep the assignation, and Kelshall realises you have betrayed him after all, what will become of you?"

She made an impatient gesture. "What can he do, in a crowded public place like this? Anyway, I do not care! Oh, Geraint, do not waste any more time! Go, while you may."

"Will you tell me one thing?" Geraint said mildly, ignoring this advice. "If you are bent upon so secret a matter as murder, why are you wearing that peculiarly conspicuous garment?"

"Cousin Roger procured it for me. I confess I do not quite like it, but I believe he wished to be certain of finding me in the crowd."

"That," remarked Geraint, "he could hardly fail to do." He put up his quizzing-glass and studied her appraisingly. "Do not think, m'dear, that I am criticising your appearance, but is not that colour a little strident? One would have thought that a man as keen-witted as Kelshall could have found a more subtle way of distinguishing his fellow conspirator, even at a masquerade."

The words put her in mind of something she had forgotten. She unfastened her domino and began to detach one of the white roses from the cluster at her breast.

"He said I was to give you this, and make sure that you wear it," she explained. "As a sort of pledge, you know, when we made the assignation."

"A charming gesture!" Again the quizzing-glass was levelled, this time at the rose. "May I ask why?"

"To make certain that it is you who walks into the trap, I suppose. With everyone masked, it is so difficult to be sure."

"Of course! How dull-witted of me! It would be disconcerting, would it not, to find that you had murdered the wrong man?" The mockery died out of his eyes, and his hands came up suddenly to cover hers as she fastened the flower into his coat. "I wonder if I *can* trust you?"

"You can!" There was a sob in her voice, and her fingers left the rose to clasp his. "Oh, believe me, you can!"

"I want to believe it," he said in a low voice. "Will you prove your good faith, Antonia?"

"Yes," she whispered. "Oh, yes! Only tell me how."

"Help me to trap Kelshall. If I can force him into the open tonight, there will be an end to his plotting. Let him think that you have deceived me, and then, when we meet at midnight, you can tell me what he means to do. Meanwhile, I will tell Mountworth what is afoot, and with his help I should be able to trap Kelshall and his minion. Will you, Antonia?"

"I will do anything you ask," she replied unsteadily, "but if you do trap them, what then?"

Geraint's lips tightened, and, masked though he was, she saw in his eyes the look of a man who would deal without mercy.

"Kelshall shall meet me," he said quietly, "and I shall kill him. This time he shall not escape. I tried to force a quarrel on him before, but he contrived to evade it and the next day left London."

She stared at him, wide-eyed. "He never told me that!"

"Did he not?" Geraint's tone was whimsical. "I dare say there is a good deal he does not tell you, m'dear. Have you not yet realised that he seeks to use you for his own purpose?"

"Yes," she replied bitterly, "I realised that long ago, but by then I was too deeply implicated to draw back. Oh, what a fool I have been!" She sighed, and, withdrawing her hands from his, stopped to pick up the mask she had dropped. "I must go, or Timothy will be suspicious, and your friends will be coming to look for you."

She was lifting the mask to her face when Geraint's hands closed once more over hers. For a moment he stood looking down into her eyes, and then he took her in his arms and kissed her, a long, hard kiss that left her breathless and trembling. At last he released her and, taking the mask, fastened it gently in place. Then he set his hands on her shoulders and looked at her with an odd little smile lifting the corners of his mouth.

"I wonder," he said softly, "whether this is the end, or the beginning? I suppose we shall know—at midnight."

His hands slid down to her wrists, he lifted them and touched her fingers with his lips. Then, turning abruptly, he left her, and his grey domino faded quickly into the shadows.

Antonia, hastening to rejoin Preston, was more thankful than ever for the mask which so completely concealed her face. Without it, she thought, she must surely have betrayed herself, for she was tingling with the memory of Geraint's arms about her, his lips on hers. For the first time she dared to let herself hope that a reconciliation between them might be possible.

Timothy was still lounging on the seat where she had left him, but he rose with unconcealed impatience as she approached. "It has taken you long enough!" he said insolently. "Were you successful?"

She nodded, too happy to resent his tone. "Yes, I was as vulgar as any Cyprian, and feigned coyness when he would have taken off my mask. He will be at our trysting-place, never fear."

"Good!" Timothy took her arm and led her along the walk. "Now let us find Sir Roger. We have not much time."

The meeting-place which Sir Roger had appointed was

at the end of one of the walls and quite close to a gate. He was waiting there, and seemed perturbed.

"Is all well?" he asked, adding, as Timothy assented: "That is something, at all events! I wish *I* could say the same." He took Antonia by the arm. "Wait here, Tim, We shall be back directly. Come, child."

"Where to?" She hung back, suddenly suspicious. "What has happened?"

"Devil take it, Antonia! Will you do as I say? If we stand here arguing, all will be lost. You will understand in a few minutes."

Reluctant, still suspicious, but afraid to refuse lest by doing so she somehow imperilled Geraint, she allowed him to lead her to the gate and out of the Gardens. A short way off a shabby-looking hackney coach was waiting. Sir Roger opened the door.

"Get in, child," he commanded. "I cannot say what I have to say in the open."

Wondering what had occurred to agitate him, who never allowed himself to betray emotion, she did as he ordered. As she entered the carriage something heavy and stifling was flung over her head, and at the same time Kelshall gave her a violent push which threw her in a heap on the floor of the coach.

She struggled desperately but unavailingly. The domino was torn from her shoulders, and her wrists and ankles bound with something soft but unyielding, and all the while the person who had thrown the covering over her head held it ruthlessly in place so that she was almost suffocated. When it was at last removed she could only gasp for breath, and before she could recover sufficiently to cry out her mask had been ripped off and a gag thrust into her mouth.

"So! It is done!" Roger's voice was carefully lowered and a trifle breathless. "And with a minimum of fuss. Accept my compliments. You were most helpful."

Dazedly Antonia lifted her head to see who had earned
his praise, and then blinked and looked again. One of her
own ball-dresses, of pale blue embroidered with silver,
was confronting her, and wearing it was a buxom young
woman, powdered, painted and patched, whom she had
some difficulty in recognising as her abigail.

Sir Roger hoisted her from her huddled position on the
floor to the seat of the coach, and propped her in a
corner. The interior of the carriage was faintly illuminated by the lamps about the entrance to the Gardens,
and a glimmer of moonlight, and she could see that he
was smiling.

"I apologize for this, my dear," he said with assured
concern. "I much dislike being obliged to resort to violence, but I cannot allow you to betray me any further to
St. Arvan. As I am sure you must have guessed, Hannah
will go in your place to meet him. I shall not harrow your
feelings by describing what will follow."

Antonia made a convulsive movement, her eyes, staring at him above the gag, eloquent of the despairing, horrified protest she was unable to utter. Hannah, who had
been arranging the scarlet domino about her shoulders
and putting on the mask, leaned forward to remove the
ear-rings from her mistress's ears.

"I'd best have these, too, sir," she said impudently. "I
don't doubt Mr. St. Arvan noticed 'em."

"By all means, Hannah! We must overlook nothing."
Sir Roger turned again to Antonia. "When our—er—
business with your husband is concluded, Hannah and her
father will return to this carriage and you will drive back
together to Brook Street. By the time you reach the
house, Timothy and Hannah will have left you, your
property will have been restored, and no one will be
aware that the scarlet domino has been worn tonight by
two different people. Your other servants, however, are
aware that *you* wore them, and as I am tolerably certain

that St. Arvan will enlist Mountworth's aid to capture me, his lordship will know it, too. In his grief for his friend, I am sure I can depend upon him to accuse you, but I need hardly point out to you the futility of accusing me in your turn."

He paused, studying her for a moment or two while the smile broadened on his lips. Then he adjusted the domino which his struggle to overpower her had disarranged, shook out his ruffles and looked at the abigail.

"Are you ready, Hannah?" he said amiably. "Then let us go. You must on no account be late for your assignation with St. Arvan."

As midnight was striking, a gentleman with a grey domino hanging loosely from his shoulders, and a white rose in his peach-coloured velvet coat, strolled towards the card-room in the pavilion at Vauxhall Gardens. His bearing was casual, but through the slits of his mask, eyes of vivid blue held a wary gleam. He seemed to be looking for someone, for he glanced about him as he walked; suddenly he paused, and then went forward in a more purposeful manner.

A tall woman in a domino of flaring scarlet silk had emerged from the card-room. The hood was drawn up over her powdered hair, and a scarlet mask lavishly trimmed with lace concealed her features, but as she turned her head there was a flash of rubies and diamonds from the ornaments in her ears. Grey Domino went briskly to her side and bowed. She turned with an eagerness tinged, it seemed, with apprehension, for she cast an anxious glance from side to side before placing her hand on his proffered arm, and as they moved away looked fearfully over her shoulder.

Once outside the pavilion Geraint would have paused,

but the Scarlet Domino shook her head and, catching his hand in hers, hurried off across the Gardens. From her haste, and the way in which she repeatedly glanced behind her as though fearing pursuit, he concluded that she had succeeded momentarily in evading her fellow conspirators, and was anxious to be out of sight before they appeared on the scene. So, reflecting that he could do nothing until she disclosed her kinsman's plans, he went with her willingly enough.

Behind them, the crimson domino which masked the identity of Lord Mountworth, emerged cautiously from the pavilion and set off in pursuit, guided by the glimmer of brilliant red disappearing along a nearby path. He strode rapidly after it, wondering with some misgiving why they were making off in such haste. He was by no means convinced that Antonia was to be trusted, and had done his utmost to dissuade his friend from staking his life on the gamble that she was.

He had gone only a short way when a tall man in a black domino, stepping unexpectedly from the shadows beneath a tree, collided with him so violently that they both staggered. Peter would have passed on with only a brief word of apology, but the other gripped him by the arm.

"Why, it is Mountworth, is it not?" said a familiar, mocking voice. "This is indeed a fortunate chance."

Peter stared hard at the speaker, and through the slits of the mask, hard, pale blue eyes ironically returned his regard.

"These masked frolics are tedious in the extreme, are they not?" Kelshall went on. "Fortunately, one can always find relief from boredom at the card-table. A few hands of picquet, my lord? It is, I believe, a game of which you are particularly fond."

The Scarlet Domino and her companion were almost out of sight. Understanding dawned suddenly in Peter's mind, and for a moment he was nonplussed by Kelshall's sheer effrontery. Not only was he preventing Peter from going to the aid of his friend; he was forcing him to provide Kelshall himself with an alibi.

A wave of unaccustomed fury swept over Mountworth, for, like many even-tempered men, he was capable on occasion of very violent anger. Before Sir Roger realised what was happening, Peter had struck him in the face with his free hand, wrenched himself from the other's involuntarily slackened grip, and floored him with a second blow. By the time Kelshall was able to collect his scattered wits, Mountworth had vanished.

Geraint, meanwhile, following his fair guide along paths which grew ever more deserted the farther they went, was conscious of a growing uneasiness. They should have been safe enough now from possible pursuit, but still the Scarlet Domino hurried on. Midnight was a popular hour for supper and there were far fewer people moving about the walks than there had been earlier; it occurred to Geraint that Kelshall had chosen his time well, and also that there was no indication that Peter was anywhere in the vicinity. He cast a glance behind him, but no crimson domino rewarded his searching gaze.

"Antonia!" he said, coming to a halt, and at once she swung round to face him. For a moment they looked at each other, and then she shook her head, laid a finger to her lips, and, taking his hand again, led him on along the path.

He wondered why she did not speak, for there could be no risk now of being overheard. There was some slight, indefinable change in her bearing which troubled him; it seemed that she carried her head less high, and moved with something less than her usual grace.

These vague suspicions were still floating tenuously in his mind when a tiny accident occurred which crystallised them into cold, hard certainty. As they went, a stray branch pulled the skirt of the scarlet domino a little to one side, revealing beneath it a silver-embroidered gown of blue. At once there flashed into his mind the memory of Antonia flinging back her cloak to unfasten the rose from her breast, flinging it back to disclose ivory-coloured brocade and satin. Whoever the Scarlet Domino he followed now might be, she was certainly not his wife.

A moment later she halted before one of the summer-houses which were scattered here and there about the Gardens, fashioned in the style of Grecian temples and the like. She set one hand on the side of the doorway and sent a searching glance all around as though to assure herself they were not observed, and then gestured in the most natural manner in the world for him to enter the building.

For a second or two he hesitated. In this remote corner of the Gardens, to which the music penetrated only faintly, there was not another human being in sight, and though the moonlight bathed the whole scene in a white radiance the interior of the summer-house was dark as the grave. A grim little smile touched his lips as the aptness of the comparison occurred to him, and he moved slowly forward to the threshold.

His next movement was entirely unexpected. He entered the building with a speed and suddenness which carried him across its entire width in one lightning movement, and he had swung about with his back to the far wall, and wrenched his small-sword from its sheath, before either the woman or the unseen presence he sensed within the summer-house had realised what he was about.

The would-be assassin did not lack courage, or perhaps it was desperation which prompted his next move. Whichever it was, Geraint saw him silhouetted against the moonlit doorway as he sprang towards him, and struck with the flat of his blade at the glimmer of steel in his hand. The weapon clattered to the floor and then the man was on him, clawing fingers reaching for his throat, and it was impossible to attempt a second thrust. Geraint dropped the sword and grappled with his assailant, knowing at once, from the man's lack of height and unexpected, wiry strength, that it was not Kelshall himself who had lain in wait for him.

Peter, pounding breathlessly along the path, found himself suddenly before a summer-house improbably designed to resemble a temple, by the doorway of which, her tall hooded figure dark against the moon-whitened wall, stood the Scarlet Domino. She had a hand at her breast, and was peering so intently into the building that she did not notice his approach. From the interior of the summer-house came unmistakably the sounds of a struggle.

Peter's sword-hilt was lost amid folds of crimson silk, and as he fumbled, cursing, to free it, two men locked together in desperate combat staggered out into the moonlight, lost their balance and pitched to the ground. Mountworth's sword came free at last, but so closely grappled were the Grey Domino and the Black that in the uncertain moonlight he did not dare to intervene.

For several moments longer the conflict continued, but at last the struggles of the Black Domino, which had been growing steadily less vigorous, ceased altogether and he lay still. After a second or two Geraint rose unsteadily to his feet, assisted by Peter's ready hand beneath his elbow.

"Geraint!" Mountworth was concerned. "Are you all right?"

St. Arvan nodded. He was breathing heavily, and stripped off his mask to wipe the sweat from his face. As he did so, the Scarlet Domino, who all the while had stood backed against the wall, staring in dismay at the fight going on almost at her feet, was roused to sudden activity. She caught up her voluminous skirts and, darting past the two men, fled with the speed of panic towards the centre of the Gardens.

Taken by surprise, they were unable to prevent her, though Mountworth made a vain grab at her as she sped past. Geraint started in pursuit, recollected that Kelshall was still at large, and plunged again into the summer-house to retrieve his sword. He found it, and something else as well, a dagger which drew blood from his fingers as they encountered it in their groping after his own weapon.

He swore, but picked it up and carried it into the moonlight, where the bright blade and inlaid hilt gleamed balefully up at him. For an instant he stood looking at it, a frown in his eyes; then he swathed his handkerchief about it and dropped it into his pocket.

Mountworth was bending over the unconscious man. He had ripped off the mask, and a pallid, unremarkable face was revealed in the moon's faint radiance.

"Kelshall himself tried to stop me following you," he said over his shoulder. "Your wife has probably gone to find him."

"That wasn't Antonia!" Geraint slid his sword back into the scabbard. "Look after this fellow, Peter. I must go after her."

Hannah raced desperately back the way she had come. This had been part of the plan, the headlong flight of the Scarlet Domino through the crowds about the boxes to the gate where the coach was waiting, and where Timothy, making his way there by a different route, was to join her; but the man who should by now be lying dead in the little temple, with his wife's dagger in his heart, was very much alive and without doubt hurrying in pursuit. The thought spurred her to even more frantic speed, and she ran on, wishing very much that the embroidered shoes which she had filched from her mistress's wardrobe were not so tight and so high in the heel.

She reached the more crowded part of the Gardens, and ventured to slacken her pace a little to look back the way she had come. The action proved to be her undoing, for while she was thus chin-on-shoulder she ran full tilt into a man in a violet domino, who was quick to take advantage of the accident by flinging both arms around her. He was the beau who had ogled Antonia during supper, now considerably the worse for drink.

"Gad's life, here's luck!" he exclaimed thickly. "The Scarlet Domino, by all that's wonderful! Thought I'd lost you, my pretty."

"Let me go, damn you!" she said furiously. "Let me go!"

"No, no!" he retorted, laughing. "We'll see what's behind that pretty mask first."

He was already fumbling for the strings when a hard, tapering heel ground viciously into his instep, and with a howl of pain he let her go. She slipped away into the crowd, leaving him to cherish his bruised foot and curse all evil-tempered females. A few moments later he was vexed even more to find himself brushed unceremoniously out of the way by a very tall and somewhat dishevelled young man with a torn grey domino hanging from his shoulders.

Geraint thrust his way with little regard for courtesy through the throng of people about the boxes, but the Scarlet Domino flitted always just out of reach. The more boisterous element in the crowd was beginning to make itself felt, and there was a good deal of rowdy horseplay going on, to the accompaniment of shrieks and laughter, while numerous inebriated gentlemen added their mite to the general uproar. Several gallants seemed inclined to take exception to Geraint's abrupt passage through their ranks, but a glance at his face was sufficient to stifle their protests in their throats, for it was plain that here was a man who would brook no opposition.

The Scarlet Domino won through the worst of the crowd while Geraint was still trapped among the merry-makers, and it seemed likely that she would make her escape, for by the time he broke free of the people about him she was already some distance ahead along the walk which led to the gate and the safety of the waiting coach. Coming towards her was a group of about eight masked men and women, and beyond them, beneath one of the trees bordering the path, a tall Black Domino stood motionless, watching her approach and that of her pursuer. There was a certain tenseness in his attitude, and below the edge of his mask, thin lips were compressed into a hard, straight line.

Whatever he was planning to do, and whatever would have happened when St. Arvan drew level with him, was suddenly brought to nothing by the hilarious group between. One of its members saw the Scarlet Domino hastening towards him with Geraint in pursuit, and had an impulse to take a hand in the game. He joined hands with his companions on either side and called to them to do the same, so that in a moment a line of laughing revellers blocked the path from side to side and her way of escape was closed. She made one frantic attempt to break through and then Geraint was beside her, his hand on her shoulder, while the line swept into a circle about them, with laughter and appropriate jests. Geraint's other hand came up and ripped the mask from her face.

"Good God!" he said blankly. "Hannah!" Then his fingers tightened on her shoulder so that she uttered a gasp of pain. "Where is my wife? By Heaven! If you have harmed her . . . !"

Hannah looked frantically to right and left. She could

follow instructions efficiently enough, but now all Kelshall's plans were overset and she and her father captives in St. Arvan's hands. Where was Sir Roger? He should have prevented Mountworth from following St. Arvan to the summer-house, but Mountworth had come; he should be at hand to help her now, but he was nowhere to be seen. A suspicion of betrayal took shape in her mind. Trust Sir Roger Kelshall to set his own safety above all considerations of loyalty. He had forgotten, it seemed, that the betrayed could betray in their turn.

"She's all right," she replied at length, looking up at Geraint. "I'll tell you where to find her. I'll tell you enough to hang Sir Roger twice over—at a price."

Alone and helpless in the coach, Antonia had lost all count of time. It might have been only a few minutes since Kelshall and Hannah left her, or it might have been hours. At first she had struggled with all her lithe young strength to free herself, but her bonds, for all their softness, were unyielding as the strongest cord. Sir Roger was taking no chances, she thought bitterly. There would be no rope-marks on her flesh tomorrow to bear out a story of abduction.

At last she gave up, utterly exhausted, and her anguished thoughts followed the conspirators back to the masquerade. Was there any chance that Geraint would see through Hannah's disguise? No, how should he, when Kelshall had been at such pains to ensure that he was expecting to meet his wife at the trysting-place? He would follow the Scarlet Domino unsuspectingly, and she would lead him to his death.

How long had she sat here alone? Perhaps the hour was already past, and in some hidden corner of the Gardens Geraint's gaiety and vigour lay stark in death, the laughter in his eyes stilled for ever. "The end," he had said, "or the beginning?" Oh, it was the end, the end of her whole world.

The door opened, and her heart gave a great lurch of horror. A tall figure sprang up into the coach, slamming the door behind him, and at the same moment the horses were put in motion and the vehicle jolted forward. She stared at him, questions clamouring in her mind, while he discarded mask and domino and tossed both on to the opposite seat. He settled his coat and rearranged his lace, which had been somewhat crushed under the domino. Then he leaned back in his corner of the coach and took out his snuff-box. He seemed quite unperturbed.

"You are wondering, no doubt," he remarked amiably, "why I, and not Timothy and Hannah, have rejoined you." He opened the box, took a pinch, and shook away the surplus with an elegant gesture. "Matters, as you have guessed, did not go quite according to plan."

He lifted the snuff to his nose and inhaled with pleasure, while Antonia sat utterly still, her gaze fixed with painful intensity on his dimly seen figure. How like him to torment her, to keep her in suspense until, but for the gag in her mouth, she would have screamed to him to tell her the truth.

"Not at all according to plan," he repeated pensively. "In fact, I am obliged to admit that St. Arvan has won the day. What became of Timothy I do not know, but when last I saw Hannah she was busily engaged in bargaining with your husband, and promising to turn informer. He had unmasked her, of course. I wonder how she betrayed herself?"

Antonia heard his voice as from a great distance, and for a few seconds her surroundings dissolved into whirling darkness, but through it all one thought sounded an exultant fanfare in her mind. Geraint was safe. He was safe, and Sir Roger owned himself defeated. How it had happened she did not for the moment know or care; the fact itself was more than sufficient.

The coach was travelling at a reckless pace. Kelshall put away his snuff-box, leaned unhurriedly towards her and in the same leisurely manner removed the gag.

"I think we can dispense with this," he remarked, "and with these tiresome bonds. I trust you did not find them too uncomfortable?"

Antonia moistened her lips. "Oh, no!" she said sarcastically. "I enjoy being bound hand and foot."

"You are in spirits, my child," he replied, fumbling with the bonds upon her wrists. "Our defeat does not seem to weigh too heavily upon you."

"Our defeat?" Her hands were free at last, and she began to rub some life back into her numbed arms. "Surely, cousin, the time for pretence is past? You know well enough that never, save for a very little while when Geraint first accused me, did I feel any desire for your murderous plans to succeed."

"Yes, I know it. You came to me that day in a fit of uncontrollable anger because St. Arvan, knowing nothing of Hannah's eavesdropping, would not believe you innocent of betraying him, but though you still wanted to punish him, the desire to see him dead faded as soon as your temper cooled. I was not in the least surprised."

She had been leaning forward to untie the bonds about her ankles, but at that she straightened up abruptly. "You were not?"

"Not in the least," he repeated. "Remember, I knew your mother, whom you so closely resemble, and once, I recollect, when she imagined that Anthony had been unfaithful to her, she tried to stab him. He managed to deflect the blow, the knife gashed his arm instead, and she was instantly overcome by remorse. The same thing, in effect, happened to you. You are besotted with St. Arvan, but because he wronged you, you desired for a short while to strike back at him. A passion for revenge, my dear! It is in the blood—the gipsy blood. A singularly futile emotion."

"I agree," she said scornfully, "though it seems to me, cousin, that I arrived at that conclusion far sooner than you did. You have cherished such an emotion for more than twenty years."

"I?" There was infinite contempt in his voice. "Do you seriously imagine that I strove so earnestly to gain control of the Kelshall fortune for no better reason than revenge? Acquit me of that, I beg! I am not Sir Charles, half crazed and senile, obsessed by hatred and living only to gratify it."

"Do you deny that you killed my father in order to become Sir Charles's heir?"

"I do not deny it. I killed him for the same reason I tried to murder your husband. Because I am in need of money. Twenty years ago it was simply my ambition to be rich instead of poor; today I am facing ruin."

She stared towards him, trying to make out his expression. "I do not believe it! The way you live . . ."

"Sham, my child, nothing but a sham. A fine façade presented to the world, and behind it nothing but duns and debts. Extravagance and unlucky speculation have brought me to the end of my resources. Good God! Do you think I would have risked everything—family, position, even life itself—if I could have seen any other way of averting disaster?"

"And you thought that if Vincent married me, you would be able to hold the purse-strings, and settle your debts with my money?"

"My dear Antonia," he replied coldly, "you flatter yourself unduly. Do you imagine I would permit my son to marry a woman of your birth, the daughter of a discredited gamester and his gipsy light-o'-love? Or that St. Arvan would have married you had he not been reduced to such desperate straits that he could not refuse? And even then Sir Charles knew better than to let him discover the truth until after the knot was safely tied."

She cringed beneath the lash of words which brought cruelly to mind the many humiliations of her childhood and girlhood, but she still had spirit enough to retort: "You can say that, even though you urged Vincent to come to Gloucestershire, to pay court to me and ask me to marry him?"

He laughed, very softly and gently, yet with something in the sound which laid a sudden chill upon her. "That was necessary in order to win your trust, to persuade you to place yourself in my hands once you inherited. I fear you would not have lived to see your wedding-day."

In spite of the warmth of the summer night, Antonia shivered. How right Sir Charles had been to distrust his kinsman; how fortunate she was to have escaped the snare spread for her. She did not doubt that Kelshall was speaking the truth, for what he said made clear a good many things which had puzzled her. She had never been able to reconcile Roger Kelshall as she knew him, cold, calculating and passionless, with the undying thirst for vengeance his actions had appeared to indicate.

For a while her thoughts were fully occupied, and since Sir Roger had also fallen silent, the clatter and jingle of their headlong progress was for a considerable interval the only sound. Slowly, however, a fresh apprehension forced itself upon her, and she peered again through the darkness at her companion.

"Where are you taking me?" she demanded.

Kelshall raised his head. "To Brook Street," he replied. "I confess that it did cross my mind to spirit you away and hold you to ransom, but I have a suspicion that St. Arvan, armed with Hannah's confession, would not submit tamely to being bled. Moreover, such a course would need time and careful preparation if it were to succeed. A wise man, Antonia, knows when his race is run."

There was a little silence; at length she said: "What will you do now?"

"I am going to escort you home," he replied, after a scarcely perceptible hesitation, "and then I shall return to my own house. You may rest assured that unless St. Arvan mishandles the situation—and I credit him with wit enough not to mishandle it—the truth will never be known." He paused, but she could find nothing to say, and was still seeking for words when he spoke again. "What of yourself, Antonia?"

"I?" She was startled. "I do not understand."

"No?" he queried with a hint of mockery. "Yet surely the question clamours for an answer. Your situation is, to say the least of it, equivocal." He paused, as though giving the matter his consideration. "You would, I think, be wise to come to terms with St. Arvan. Your attempt to warn him tonight will have shown that you are eager to make amends, and his own conduct during the past few months has not been so blameless that you have nothing to forgive. There has been fault upon both sides."

There was another, longer pause, and then she said in a small voice: "You suggest, in fact, that I bargain with him?"

"Precisely!" Sir Roger seemed pleased by such ready understanding. "You must remember that you are bound to each other for life, and so it is only prudent to come to some arrangement whereby you may live amicably together. I am sure that you will be able to persuade him to let bygones be bygones. He will not change, of course, but you have one inestimable advantage over your rivals. You are his wife."

She made no reply and he did not press the matter, for he was well aware of the insidious power of an innuendo left to prick and rankle in the mind, and the seeds of doubt, sown now, might well make impossible a complete reconciliation between her and her husband. It was a dubious satisfaction, but the only one he could salvage from the ruin of all his hopes.

When Sir Roger arrived at his own house, having set Antonia down in Brook Street, he went straight to his study and locked the door behind him. He lit the candles in the branched silver holders on the desk, and then sat down and took out writing materials. For a considerable while only the scratching of his pen disturbed the stillness, and the candles had burned low by the time he laid it aside. He folded and sealed the packet, and wrote a direction upon it in his elegant, flowing hand. Then he unlocked a drawer and took from it a small, silver-mounted pistol, which he proceeded to load with his usual unhurried calm.

When it was done, he laid the weapon down, took out his snuff-box and with great deliberation helped himself to a pinch. The house was very silent, but as he returned the box to his pocket, there arose from the street outside the quavering voice of the Watch calling the hour, and informing the city that it was a fine night and all was well. A slight, ironic smile touched Sir Roger's lips, and he put out a steady hand for the pistol.

Antonia went slowly upstairs to her dressing-room. It was deserted, for Hannah, who should have been waiting there to help her mistress prepare for bed, was still elsewhere, endeavouring, no doubt, to extricate herself from the consequences of her part in the plot against Geraint's life. It was not to be expected that she would return.

Antonia lit the candles on the dressing-table, exchanged her crumpled, tight-laced ball-dress and cumbersome hooped petticoats for a wrapper of flowered silk, and then sat down before the mirror and stared unseeingly at her reflection. Her first rush of exultation at Sir Roger's admission of defeat was clouded now by apprehension of what the sequel to it might be. Geraint had said that if Kelshall were trapped, their quarrel might be settled at sword-point, and though there seemed little danger that Sir Roger could prevail, the consequences would be very serious indeed if he died at Geraint's hands. Although affairs of honour frequently took place, duelling was against the law, and it would go hard with a swordsman of Geraint's reputation if he killed a man so many years his senior. At best, he would be obliged to fly the country; at worst—Antonia shivered, unable to face the thought of what the worst would mean.

She could derive no comfort, either, from turning to contemplation of her own situation. Sir Roger's words had already begun their poisonous work, and the suggestion that she should try to strike a bargain with her husband lingered distastefully in her mind. Kelshall had implied that, just as Geraint had amused himself with other women while his wife plotted against his life, so he would be ready to forget their differences now that her schemes had come to nothing. It did not, hinted Sir Roger, matter greatly to St. Arvan one way or the other. Perhaps that was true, and if he were willing to forget the events of the past few months, she knew that she ought to be profoundly grateful, but that, cried her heart despairingly, was not enough. She wanted to know that his love for her was as deep as hers for him; to recapture the happiness they had known in the springtime.

She was roused from her unhappy thoughts by the sound of a hasty footstep outside, and sprang up to turn apprehensively towards the door. It opened, and Geraint came quickly in, to stride across and grip her by the shoulders, looking anxiously into her face.

"Antonia, are you all right? They did not hurt you?" She shook her head, and his hold on her relaxed; he said with a wry smile: "Hannah told me where to find the hackney-coach in which you were imprisoned, but when I came in search of you the damned thing had gone. I knew it must be Kelshall's doing, and feared he might intend holding you as hostage for Hannah and her father."

"He told me that he did think of holding me to ransom," she replied unsteadily, "But that since Hannah had confessed he would have little hope of succeeding." She looked anxiously up at him. "Is the danger really over, Geraint? Cousin Roger said that his race was run, but I did not know whether I could believe him."

He nodded. "Yes, it is over."

"And there will be no meeting between you?"

"No. This is the better way." Geraint took her hand and led her to the sofa and made her sit down. "Hannah told me the whole story, and when Preston realised that the truth was out, he confirmed it. Peter is obtaining from them written confessions, properly signed and witnessed, and with those documents in my possession I shall hold Kelshall at my mercy. He dare not, for his life's sake, make any further attempt against me." He paused, looking down at her with a faint frown. "Did you know that he is on the verge of ruin?"

"He told me on the way home," she admitted in a low voice. "Geraint, will there be a great scandal?"

"Not of my making. That was part of my agreement with Preston. In exchange for the confessions, I have given my word to make none of this public. He is devoted to Kelshall, and as anxious to protect him as to purchase freedom for himself and his daughter." He put his hand into his pocket and took out the ruby and diamond ear-rings. "Here are your trinkets. I told Hannah she might keep the gown, for I did not think you would care to wear it again."

"Indeed I would not," she agreed emphatically, taking the jewels, "but I am thankful to have these safe. I could not bear to lose them."

"Because they were your first gift to me," she added in her thoughts, and wondered if he remembered it, too. If he did, he made no comment, but instead said gravely:

"This was not the first time that Hannah had assumed your identity. Kelshall knew he would have difficulty in compelling you to take an active part in his murderous game, and so he resolved to incriminate you without your knowledge."

Sitting down beside her, he told her of the men who had been paid to set upon him, and what he and Peter had learned from their leader. "When the fellow told me a woman had hired him, and described her to me, I believed what Kelshall intended to be believed—that it was you." He was silent for a moment and then added in a dry tone: "It was on the day after that I sent you back to Gloucestershire."

"The next day?" A hand to her mouth, Antonia stared at him, realising how blatantly false her confession and her offer of help must have sounded to him in the light of what he had been told. "Merciful Heaven! No wonder you would not believe me!"

For the first time she allowed herself to think of what they had said to each other that day, seeing how with every word she had damned herself more completely in his eyes. Then a curious contradiction in his more recent behaviour occurred to her, and she looked at him with a puzzled frown.

"Yet tonight, at Vauxhall, you *were* prepared to trust me. Why?"

He shrugged. "I believed you were convinced at last

that your danger at Kelshall's hands was as great as my own, and since the whole damnable situation had to be resolved somehow I was prepared to gamble on your good faith. When I realised that the Scarlet Domino who met me outside the card-room was not you, I knew that my judgment had been sound, and that you were to be as much a victim of the plot as I."

"I see!" Antonia spoke in a whisper, and bowed her head to hide the dismay in her eyes. So he still believed her to be governed by self-interest, and there seemed no hope of ever convincing him otherwise. A sense of utter hopelessness engulfed her, and her eyes filled with tears she was too tired and wretched to hold back. Dreading pity more than anything, she made a tremendous effort to keep her voice steady as she said, without looking up: "I recognised my own danger long since, but thank Heaven this horror is over at last, for both of us." She paused, took a deep breath, and with one final effort added unsteadily: "May we not talk of this in the morning? I am very tired."

"I know," he said gently, "but there is one thing yet to be explained. What you did tonight could have been prompted by a desire to save yourself, but there is something else, which cannot. This, Antonia."

He held his hand out in front of her; across it lay an antique dagger, its hilt inlaid with turquoise and gold.

"Preston tried to use this on me tonight," Geraint went on quietly. "Later he told me how it came to be in his possession. In God's name, Antonia, why did you do such a thing?"

The brief delay had tried her precarious composure too far. The dagger blurred and swam in a mist of tears as she said with a catch in her voice: "I had to stop him. That was the only thing I could think of, to kill him and then myself. But he guessed what I meant to do."

"Thank God he did!" Geraint's own voice was unsteady. He tossed the dagger aside and caught her in his arms. "My darling, how could you think I would have wanted safety at such a price? Life would mean nothing at all without you."

"I thought you no longer cared," she sobbed. "Oh, Geraint, how can you forgive me? What I did was beyond forgiveness."

"Even if it were," he said ruefully, "I drove you to it with my damned suspicion. We could spend the rest of our lives, love, apportioning the blame and seeking forgiveness of each other—and much it would profit us! We are going to put the whole accursed business behind us, and go back to the moment when I left you to ride to Barnet."

"If that were possible!" Antonia's voice was still choked with tears. "Oh, if only it were!"

"It is possible because we shall make it so." His hold tightened, crushing her against him; the blue eyes smiled down into hers, loving her, teasing her, daring her to defy him. She started to speak, and he bent his head to kiss her lightly on the lips, stifling whatever she was about to say. "Hush, now! We will talk of it, if talk we must, in the morning."

FAWCETT CREST
BESTSELLERS